The Mysterious Island

CHRIS PIERCE

Fulton Books, Inc.
Meadville, PA

Published by Fulton Books 2021

ISBN 978-1-63860-142-5 (paperback)
ISBN 978-1-63860-143-2 (digital)

Printed in the United States of America

PART I

This story is a long-forgotten tale that has been passed down from generation to generation. Eventually, it was written down, but no one knows when that happened. Some of the tale has not been translated or has been lost to time. This book has the parts that were translated and placed together in order of events.

Scholars argue about the time period when this tale took place. Many of them like to believe it started during the medieval times in England. Others argue the tale took place much earlier, but written down during the medieval period in history. The location of the tale has been never been found, and scholars argue where they think the castle is located. You can search for the location yourself, but it is all just dead ends. All we know is that there is a castle and a nearby desert. It doesn't matter when or where it took place; it just matters that it did take place.

CHAPTER 1

A King, a Queen, and a Mysterious Old Wizard

Once upon a time, a long time ago, in a not-so-distant land, there lived a king and queen. They ruled justly, with great honor and wisdom. The kingdom prospered and grew in every way. The people of the kingdom loved their king and queen. All was well, except for one disheartening thing; the king and queen were unable to bear any children. There was great mourning in the palace with each passing year because as the king grew older, his hope for an heir lessened. Without an heir, his kingdom would fall into the hands of another.

The king and queen were average people. Both were average height, and both had brown hair and brown eyes. The queen's eyes were a darker shade of brown. They wore the typical garments a king and queen would wear. Their robes were a mix of white, blue, and purple, and they always wore the robes while they were in the castle. The queen loved wearing dresses that she got from different countries around the world. Her favorite ones were the white and blue dresses of Italy. They both sounded like how the average British royalty would sound.

One day, a few months later, on a cloudy and gloomy autumn day, an old man was walking by the castle. This strange-looking man was small. He stood about four and a half feet tall and was dressed in a very well-worn, almost-holey, midnight-blue robe that was lined with small white images of wolves. The sleeves were embroidered with white crescent moons around the lining. Dust fell off the bottom hem when he stopped at the castle entrance. The inside of the robe was made from wolf fur. He also wore a hat that was made from wolf hide and was lined with images of a crescent white moon. He had lived many years, appearing to be close to 120 years old or more, but no one really knew for sure. He had a long gray beard that went halfway down his chest and long, braided, gray hair that flowed all the way down his back. He had large eyes that were colored a dark midnight blue. His face was old and wrinkled, with some dirt-stains caked in the valleys of his wrinkles. He carried a large walking stick, and he walked with a limp on his right side. He stood with his shoulders hunched over. The king and queen were outside the castle gates as he slowly limped by. The queen was upset and crying tears of sadness.

The old man looked puzzled at the crying and asked, "What is wrong, Your Royal Majesty?"

"It is a private matter. You would not be able to help us anyway," the king bluntly and rudely answered back to the man. "Be on your way."

"Are you sure? If it pleases Your Majesties, I can help with any kind of problem. It looks to me that the queen has a problem," the man said to the king while looking inquisitively at the queen.

"Do you really think you can help the queen in a private matter?" the king challenged firmly with a hearty laugh. "You look like you can't even take care of yourself."

"Calm yourself," the queen said to the king. "Let us see if the man can help us," she said with some hope that was lost a minute ago. She looked at the old man and said, "We have no heirs to our throne. We cannot have any children. We have been trying for years, but to no avail. How would you be able to help us?"

The man happily smiled, but with keenness in his voice, his eyes glanced toward the sky, and he proudly answered, "I can help with that, and I will always help my queen and king. I have a great and powerful magic, a magic that will be able to help your majesties."

"That didn't answer our question, *how* can you help us?" the king asked and then quietly said with sadness, "As my queen said, we have tried to have children for many years, with no success. We fear greatly that our noble kingdom will be another's. When that happens, we fear for the people. We rule them justly and with great honor, and we fear the next king will not do so."

"Magic is how I will help you," answered the man. "I will use my magic for a small price. You will have children and have an heir to your throne, an heir that will keep your kingdom forever."

"Who and what are you?" questioned the queen with puzzled concern.

"I am Ulric, a wizard from the long-lost wolf tribe," the old man answered.

The wolf tribe has never been located, but a few sightings and markings have shown that they really do exist. Legend says they were a group of great wizards that lived with wolves, deep in the highest and unreachable mountains. Petroglyphs have recently been found in caves within these alleged mountains, showing an old man standing over what appears to be an island with a flower growing out of the center of the island. No one can figure out what it means, but archeologists keep trying to figure out what it is telling them.

"What is your small price, Ulric the Wizard?" the king asked with serious scorn in his voice.

"In the Cave of the Great Wolf grows a flower, a flower with mystical powers. I need that flower to make the spell. Yet I am too old and frail to travel the path to the cave. If you can get me that flower, you will have your children. I promise," Ulric answered with a sincere voice.

The king, fighting through a laugh, playfully asked, "What does this flower look like? We have lots of flowers in the castle. You can have any of those."

Ulric looked annoyed, but answered, "This is a special flower. It is about two hands tall with light, almost-glowing, green, oval-shaped leaves, a dark-green stem, eleven midnight-blue petals, and a bright, glowing red center."

"What is so special about a flower?" questioned the king. "Why do we want to risk the life of anyone to get this flower?"

"It holds great and mighty magical properties. The flower is the source of *all* my magic, the great and powerful magic of the wolf tribe. When I obtain the flower, I can do anything magical, such as you and the queen having children, the heir to your throne, forever."

"Would you care to place your life on this?" the king asked, trying to sound smart.

Ulric answered with all his wisdom and dignity, "Yes. I will die to prove to you that this magic is real and *will* work."

"Good. I will send my bravest knight to gather this flower for you. If this is a trick, or if my knight is injured on this journey, it is *you* who will pay the ultimate price," answered the king with a stern warning while waving his finger toward Ulric.

"So be it," said Ulric, looking harshly at the king. "I will do your will."

Ulric handed the king a map to the Cave of the Great Wolf. The location of the cave was kept secret, and it still cannot be found today. The king awarded Ulric by placing him in shackles and placing him inside a cold and damp cell for the night. Ulric rolled his eyes because deep down he knew his magic would be able to free him at any moment.

Early the next day the knight left alone on the journey. It would take the knight about half the day to get to the cave. The king expected the knight to be back by sundown. To make sure that Ulric was not up to any tricks, the king kept him bound in the dungeon for the day. Ulric, being of old age, just complied with the king's wishes.

The knight wore his best armor for the quest he was going on. The magnificent silver armor shone brightly in the sun. His sword swung softly at his side as his horse rode off.

The journey was uneventful. Nothing happened. The knight followed the map. He followed the steep path up the mountain and entered the cave. The flower was growing out of the ground inside the cave in a spot where the sun was shining through the roof of the cave. The knight dug up the flower and put it in a leather bag on the opposite side of the sword. He left the cave and followed the path down the mountain and back to the castle. He did think that he heard a wolf howling in the middle of the day, but that would be unusual, so he didn't pay much attention to the sound.

Just as the sun was about to set, the brave knight rode to the castle gate. He was holding the bag with the flower inside. The flower looked like a small glowing star from a distance. As the knight entered the castle, the king quickly summoned for Ulric. Within a few minutes, one of the guards dragged Ulric to the throne room, forcing him to face the king.

Gently handing the flower to Ulric, the king said in an untrusting tone, "Here is your flower. Our end of the bargain is done. Now make good with your promise." He signaled the guards to keep a watch on Ulric.

Ulric prepared himself for the spell and spoke quietly to the king and queen, "Thank you, Your Majesty. I need you and the queen to quietly sit down in front of me."

The king and queen reluctantly did as Ulric requested. The guards slowly drew their swords, just in case this was a trick. Ulric waved his hands through the air and moved his mouth as if he was talking, but no words came out of his mouth. Some midnight-blue-colored dust magically appeared in the air and fell like snowflakes on the heads of the king and queen.

"Nine months from now, you will have twins, one boy and one girl. The boy will be born first, and his name shall be Az Rex, meaning he will be a powerful king and leader. The girl shall be named Karisma, for she will be a great helper to all she meets. You shall raise them to be people of high esteem and honor. You shall also continue to lead your kingdom with justice and honesty. Do not follow evil desires which will tempt you. If you do not follow these commands, your offspring will perish and you be left with nothing and the kingdom will vanish forever."

After Ulric finished his speaking to the king and queen, a blue mist fell from the sky and slowly covered him. When the mist settled on the ground, Ulric had vanished into thin air.

The king had the guards search the whole kingdom and surrounding area for Ulric, but with no avail. The king ordered the guards to keep a close lookout for Ulric, just in case this was a trick to get the flower for him.

As the months went on, the queen started to show that she was pregnant, just like Ulric had proclaimed. The king and queen, finally trusting the story which was told by Ulric, prepared the royal nursery for two babies. They hired midwives to help them raise the children because ruling a kingdom and being parents was too hard. With each day, the excitement inside the kingdom grew.

Nine months after the day of Ulric's magic spell, the queen finally gave birth to the twins. The boy named Az Rex was first, followed by the girl named Karisma. Thy boy looked like the king, and the girl looked like the queen. That night the king threw a great celebration for the kingdom. A large feast was prepared for everyone, and fireworks were shot off most of the night. Ulric, the great wizard, never showed up to see his work.

CHAPTER 2

Wars and a Creation of an Island

The king and queen loved being parents to the newborns, but they really didn't like the hard work that came along with raising the twins. The king wished that Az Rex could be a teenager so he could take him on some kingly adventures. The queen wished that they could raise the children themselves so she could take a few more trips and still fit into her dresses. Overall, they were happy, but they couldn't find the words or actions to show they were happy. Az Rex liked to sleep a lot, and Karisma was always looking around and watching people. People loved her deep blue eyes. The babies loved to be with each other.

Before long, the babies grew into toddlers and ran around the castle. Az Rex grew brave. He loved to climb anything and then jump off, landing perfectly and never hurting himself. By the time he was three, he enjoyed fighting with the king's knights. He had a real, but tiny-sized, sword. He would always lose in the end, mainly due to his size and strength, but he always gave a great fight. He longed for the day when he would win the fight. Karisma was quiet, but at the same time, she was very out going with people. She enjoyed helping anyone, whether they needed it or not, for any reason. Many times she would sneak out of the castle and to the king's market just so she could help people choose the good vegetables and carry the baskets for the older people in the kingdom. The people would always smile and take Karisma's choices. She was never wrong in her choices, and she wasn't afraid to voice her quiet opinion.

By the time the kids turned ten years old, Az Rex gained a lot of strength, the strength of a great and mighty warrior, and he also cultivated great skills in leadership. He perfected his skill in all forms of sword-fighting. He mastered the art of single sword-fighting, could two-sword fight with the best of them, and could also staff fight with the mightiest of them. He could and would beat the king's knights regularly in every kind of combat. Karisma would always be at Az Rex's side, giving him any help that he would need. She would have a drink or a bandage ready at all times. It was also known by this age, Karisma would become a beautiful princess, and Az Rex felt that it was his need to protect her. Young boys would ride by on their horses and fall off as they rode by as they stared at her. It was comical, and Az Rex would always laugh out loud. She had long dark hair, and her skin was tanned, which was unusual for royalty. She had a very proper British accent when she spoke and was always very polite. She also had the most beautiful midnight-blue eyes that anyone had ever seen. She learned very quickly how to use her eyes to get whatever she wanted; all it took was that special, almost-enhancing look. Az Rex was the typical-looking boy, other than being strong; he had short brown hair which was always messy. His eyes were dark brown, just like his father's. His skin was white and pasty.

By the time Karisma was thirteen, the boys couldn't keep their eyes off of her. Kingdoms from far away started to hear stories and rumors about her and her beauty. Knights and princes started to come to visit the king and queen with one goal, arranging a future marriage. Az Rex was always near, and he kept a very close ear, just in case she needed his protection. A few young knights would go home with bruises and some broken bones just from trying to kiss her cheek. If she didn't want a kiss, Az Rex was there to set them straight. He never lost when it came to defending his sister.

When she was sixteen, small battles started to occur near the kingdom. The fights were to see who would have the first right to ask for the marriage of Karisma because her father never made a formal arrangement for a marriage. A legend was born and started to grow rather fast about Karisma's beauty. The stories always started with her eyes. Her beauty would soon be referred to as "a beauty that would start wars." Many kingdoms would fall and never be seen or heard from again while other kingdoms grew in power and might just to have the opportunity to ask Karisma's father that one simple question, "Will Karisma become my wife?"

Az Rex would watch and wonder why someone would want to marry a girl. There were so many adventures to be a part of. He could never see himself wanting to marry someone. He did want to make sure his sister was safe.

When Karisma was nineteen, the king and queen had a surprise birth of triplet boys. The queen never felt pregnant, but she looked like she gained weight. She thought she was well past her time to have children, and having triplets was almost too much. The boys were kept hidden from all due to the continuous wars. The queen did not want the newborn boys to be targeted for someone to use against them for a victory in the war. Karisma heard rumors that she had new brothers, but she never got a chance to see them. The queen wished that their identities be kept secret in hope that they could grow up in a place without war. She hired the same midwives to raise the newborn babies.

Az Rex made his legendary sword when he was nineteen. The sword was about six feet long. It was sharpened on both sides and made a sharp hook at the top. The hook allowed him to make kills faster when he was in battle. Instead of a stab wound, the hook would grab the victim and cause more damage when he pulled the sword out. The sword was made of silver, and the hilt was made of white gold. He had diamonds placed at the top of the hilt. He, like his sister, never saw his newborn brothers. He was too busy going on adventures and protecting his sister to worry about newborn brothers. Also, this year, Az Rex found a secret lover. She was from a rival kingdom. If anyone found out, she would be killed by his parents, and he would be killed by her parents.

Karisma finally reached the age of twenty. Her beauty increased, as did the war. There was no end in sight. A kingdom would be defeated, and then another kingdom would join the war. Karisma would send supplies to try to help the brave warriors, but it only made the battles worse. The knights would start to fight over Karisma's gifts. She would beg for the fighting to stop and vowed to never marry anyone, no matter the outcome. She didn't want people to get hurt, and she really didn't want people killed because they wanted to marry her. She was a helper and wanted to help them.

At twenty, Az Rex started to become jealous of his sister. His father spent all day watching the war for her hand in marriage, and he never noticed how much Az Rex grew in strength and knowledge. His most proud accomplishment was done just after his birthday. He found his lover's kingdom had a secret gold mine and raided it himself. He killed all the guards, captured all the workers, and stashed all the gold in his own secret cave. Az Rex showed his lover his gold one summer evening. He planned to show what he had and also propose to her, hoping they could leave and find a kingdom to move to so they could escape the danger. Instead, her father followed her, and Az Rex struck him down. She ran off, never to be seen again. He slowly became rich and powerful as he raided more kingdoms. It was easy since most were fighting over his sister. Kingdoms around the area knew who he was, but he longed for his father to know him.

Ulric became bitterly upset about the great worldwide war just for a marriage proposal. He slowly and sadly made his way to Karisma's castle. There he confronted the king.

"What are you doing? Did you forget what I commanded you when I cast the spell to allow you to have children? Why do you let this pointless and unjust war continue? You have the authority to stop it. Yet you keep letting innocent people die. Your daughter is begging for this war to stop. You need to hear her words and stop this immediately."

"You gave us this beautiful daughter. Remember, you did this to us. The way I see it, it is entirely your fault. We should arrest you for starting the war, but instead, we thank you. The kingdom that wins this war will give us all they have just for their opportunity to marry my daughter, Karisma. She will *help us* to become the richest and most powerful kingdom in the entire world," the king greedily answered while in his mind he was scheming for a way to get more power. "You told us that our heirs would be powerful. You didn't tell us that their power would make us rich and powerful as well."

With those words, Ulric quickly stormed out of the castle. After he exited the door, a deafening wolf's howl echoed throughout the entire kingdom. He transformed into the misty blue cloud. The cloud slowly floated east to the middle of the open ocean. The cloud landed very softly on the water where Ulric rematerialized, standing on the water in the middle of the ocean. There he took the mystical flower out of his robe and plucked a petal off. He dropped the petal toward the water. As the petal slowly floated to the water, he raised his hands high and toward the sun. He looked toward the crescent moon, which was a sliver but visible on the eastern horizon. As he looked at the moon, his mouth started to move, just as if he was saying something; but once again, no words came out. He chanted for about ten minutes, and then Ulric clapped his hands loudly together. The sound of the clap brought forth a violent earthquake that shook the whole earth, causing a mountain to rise out of the ocean.

The mountain slowly grew into a whole but small mountain range. A few minutes later, more land appeared, and a lush forest grew to the north of the mountains. More land continued to rise out of the water, and to the west, grassy plains slowly appeared. In the center of the island, a small hut suddenly appeared. In the southern portion of the mountain range, a glassy-looking lake was formed. The lake's water was colored brilliant midnight blue. It was dark and extremely still, but the reflection of the water shone like a brand-new polished mirror. On the north shore of the lake stood a castle tower. Inside the tower, there was a long and winding stairway. At the halfway point up the stairs, a window looked south, toward the beautiful lake. At the top of the stairway was a large wooden door led to a single room at the top of the tower. Birds started to fly around the island, fish were jumping in the streams that divided the forest, plains, and mountains, and animals, large and small, started to roam the island. Ulric clapped his hands together one more time, and he floated above the island. He looked down at his new creation and smiled greatly.

"The war *will* end," he screamed into the starry sky as the night was filled with numerous thunderous wolf howls.

CHAPTER 3

The End of the War

Ulric transformed back into the mystical blue cloud and began his slow trip back to the castle. This time he traveled east so he could travel around the world and see the carnage of the raging war. He sadly gazed at the world below and looked at how war-torn the world became. Large tears fell like rain from the cloud as he saw all the dead men lying on the ground. That is not all that he saw. He also saw the earth was dying. The grass was gone. Trees were lifeless and colored a grayish brown. No birds flew around the world. No wild animals were seen. As the tears landed softy on the ground, new grass would suddenly sprout and grow.

"The world needs to be healed, and it starts with ending the war for the marriage of Karisma," he cried out loud in a sadden voice. "The king did not listen to my warning, and he became full of greed and has started a lust for power."

The cloud of mist slowly and mythically descended toward the castle. As the blue mist entered the main entrance, Ulric transformed back into his human form.

He quickly walked, with his slow limp, to the king who was watching the battle rage in front of his castle, and firmly demanded, "End this war now, or I will. You have not listened to my warning, and it ends today."

The king turned to face Ulric and arrogantly laughed as he said, "Why, what are *you* going to do? Sprinkle more of that flower dust on my head? You know as well as I, the war will end when someone takes Karisma as their wife. Both kingdoms will profit greatly from this marriage. This is and has been done with great honor because we are helping a kingdom which cannot match this one in power and might."

Ulric, red with fury, thundered in a stern and serious voice, "I will take Karisma away to a place where you will never find her. You will not even go looking for her because you will not even remember her. Your daughter will be gone from you forever. Peace will be established, and you will be left with nothing. Now, listen to my final warning. You have become greedy, arrogant, and you have a great lust for a power that is not yours to have. You forgot how to rule your kingdom with great honor. I give you until sundown tomorrow to end this war. If not, all I say will happen."

After Ulric commanded this to the king, he snapped his fingers and disappeared into thin air.

The king laughed.

"He will not, and cannot, do anything to stop us. He is an old and senile man who thinks he is a great wizard. I will have him arrested, locked up, and beheaded for our entertainment if he tries to do or stop anything," the king said to the queen.

Fear filled the queen's eyes, but the king put his arm around her and reassured her that nothing could happen.

"Maybe we should stop and listen to him. Listen to what he says. He has been right for over twenty years. The war is getting out of hand. There is nothing left in the world, and the whole world is involved in this war. We will have nothing left to gain if the world tears itself apart like this," the queen pleaded, with great concern in her voice.

"Nothing can happen, and nothing will happen. Not the kingdom, but the world will become Az Rex's. He will become the most powerful king and ruler in the world, just as the crazy old wizard foretold to us those twenty years ago. Nothing will be able to stop Az

Rex. He will be invincible," the king arrogantly bragged to all that were in earshot of them. "My heir's kingdom will live forever."

The battle came even closer to the castle that night, closer than any other night. Karisma sadly stared out of her window, and through the moonlight, she saw many knights engaged in sword battles. Sparks flew off their armor when the swords connected with a loud cling in the clear night. She was very scared and wished the fighting would just stop. She looked up at the moon, which was full and dark blue in appearance. It was a sight that she had never been seen before, and she was sure that no one else had seen anything like this before. There was a blue haze that surrounded the moon and seemed to touch the ground. Karisma stared into the haze. She begged the moon to stop the war. She felt sorry for causing such a war. A vision appeared in the mist that looked like a tower and some sort of monster floating in a lake. She thought she was seeing things, but she couldn't turn away from the vision. She quickly blinked her eyes and shook her head. The image of the tower slowly transformed into an image of a large howling wolf. She blinked her eyes a second time. This time the vision disappeared from the moon. Full of fear and not knowing what she saw, Karisma quickly retreated to her bed and hid her eyes not wanting to discover what the image meant. After of what seemed like hours of tossing and turning, she fell asleep for the rest of the night.

The next day came rather quickly. Karisma looked out her window to see if the visions were her imagination or if something was there. What she saw was her father outside, standing next to the ongoing battle, watching the knights fight to their deaths.

He was shouting at the battling men, egging them on, "Who is going to win the war? Who wants to marry my daughter and become a powerful king? She is starting to grow older each day, and beauty only lasts for a short time. You might want to hurry and win the war soon before it is too late, before she gets too old for marriage."

This day seemed strange from the start. The strangest thing was how fast the day seemed to go by. It felt like an hour went by, and the sun started to slowly set. A loud howling wolf could be heard off in the distance.

Karisma continued to be haunted by her visions and pleaded and begged with her father, "Please, Father, listen to me. The war has gone on long enough. It needs to be stopped, and stopped now. Too many innocent people have suffered and died. I don't want this for them or for me."

The king laughed softly, looked at her, and replied, "This war is all for you. I cannot stop it. The men chose to fight for you. I did not start the war, and I will not end it. Our kingdom has benefited greatly due to this war. The winner will get the ultimate prize; they get to marry you. You will be a queen someday and rule over the land. You can say that this war is for you and for Az Rex. The kingdom has been and will continue to be expanded and strengthened, all for you."

Karisma responded quickly and wisely, "You are lying, Father. I know how all this works, that Az Rex will become king. He was born first and a male. He will take over your throne and kingdom when you and Mother pass on. I will be a slave to serve Az Rex. I never asked for a war. I never asked to be married. End this war now. I do not want to marry the victor, or marry anyone. I'd rather go live by myself with wolves than be a slave to your kingdom."

The instant that she finished ranting to her father, Ulric suddenly appeared out of nowhere and forcibly yet politely demanded to the king, "Your Majesty, your time is up. Are you going to end this war, your great and honorable majesty? What is your decision? You must choose now."

"I gave you my final and honorable answer yesterday. Did you forget, you old and senile man?" The king signaled for his guards. "Arrest this man, lock him up, and prepare the guillotine for an execution. Tomorrow at sunrise, Ulric the Wizard will pay for his crimes against the kingdom," the king sternly ordered.

As the guards picked up their swords to arrest Ulric, the whole room suddenly became full of a blue hazy mist. No one could see six inches in front of their face. A cyclone of wind blew inside the castle and swept Karisma away. She didn't have time to make a sound, and she vanished, never to be seen in the kingdom again.

After the haze finally lifted, the king looked around the room.

Then he looked toward Ulric and said, "Who are you, my good man? Why are you inside my castle? Is there anything that my queen and I can help you with?"

Ulric looked in the direction of the king and never answered the king's questions; he just stared at the king, just like a wolf would when hunting his prey. Ulric turned and started to slowly limp out of the castle. As he exited, he clapped his hands together once high above his head, and the battle suddenly stopped. Each knight turned into a blue mist and disappeared. Each man had no memory of what happened as they appeared at their own castles. All knowledge of a girl named Karisma was gone.

Ulric spent the rest of the night repairing all that was damaged. He traveled around the world, replanting forests, reseeding grassy plains, cleaning the polluted water, and placing birds and animals back around the earth. He restored all the kingdoms back to those who lost. The brave and dead men were revived and put back inside their castles, with no memory of the events that happened. Everything was put back to the way it was before Karisma was born. Az Rex and his three newborn brothers were all the king and queen had left. Karisma's room was just an empty room that was used to store extra weapons. Az Rex felt empty inside like he lost something, but he had no idea what the loss was. This feeling of loss continued to haunt him each day.

CHAPTER 4

A New Place

Karisma appeared in an unfamiliar room. Panic set inside her. She looked around and didn't recognize a thing. Karisma closed her eyes, hoping this nightmare she was facing was a dream and that she would awaken soon back in her own bed in her own room. When she got the courage to open her eyes, what she saw was a bright full moon shining over a lake. The reflection was perfect. The moon was so bright she could see the reflection of a tower, the place where she was. Karisma quickly whipped around and saw a large wooden door that was open. She fled out the door to the top of the stairway and sprinted down. About halfway down the stairway was a window that she took only a short moment to look out. She saw what looked like a wolf running along the shoreline of a lake. She rushed down the rest of the stairs and out of a door at the bottom of the stairs. Karisma looked around and found herself on the shore of the lake.

Karisma walked along the lake, trying to calm herself and focus on her situation. Her eyes darted from one direction to the other, trying to take everything in.

"Where am I?" she questioned out loud, still hoping she would wake up.

"You are on the shore of Kingsbridge Lake," a voice was heard answering her.

Karisma jumped in fear, and her heart started to race.

"Who said that? Where are you?"

"It is I," was heard from a voice in the trees that ran along the shoreline. Karisma squinted and peered toward the trees. A wolf started to slowly make his way toward her. Karisma looked with fear. "Do not worry, I will not hurt you," the wolf reassured Karisma.

The wolf was large by wolf standards. Its fur was as white as a fresh snowfall in the middle of winter. It had a black nose, and its midnight-blue eyes were focused on Karisma. As the wolf came closer to her, Karisma thought back to her visions from the night before. *Could this be the same wolf that I saw?* she thought.

A blue mist slowly started to appear around the wolf. The mist started to lift, and the wolf changed into an old man.

"Hello, my name is Ulric. I am the wizard that made this island, and I also created you."

Karisma, with a very surprised and dumfounded look on her face, calmly said, "What do you mean *'created me?'* I was born of a king and queen."

Ulric told Karisma the story of her parents, how they ruled justly; how they had no heirs to the throne; how they wanted children. He told her of how he cast a spell for her parents to have the twins, Az Rex and herself. He told Karisma of the war and how the king was told to end the war. The punishment for not stopping the war was losing her.

"Do my parents remember me?" Karisma asked.

"No. They will not have any memory of you. The war is ended. Kingdoms have been restored, and the dead have been brought back to their place before you were born."

"My brother, is he still there? Will he remember me?" Karisma teared up as she asked Ulric this question.

"Yes. Your brother is still there. He needs to mature and not follow in the footsteps of your father if he wants to rule. Like your parents, he will not have any knowledge of you. You have been taken away from them," Ulric answered.

"What am I to do here all alone in a secluded tower next to a lake?" Karisma continued to question.

"I knew your father could not keep his promise. I created you for one purpose, to watch this island and protect the magic of it. You were created to become a great wizard of the wolf tribe. You have the ability to stay calm and adjust to any kind of situation without feeling panic." Ulric paused a moment and waited for Karisma to respond. Her response came in the form of her nodding. "Magic, you are thinking about the magic I speak of. You will learn how to use this magic, for I will teach you." Karisma smiled slightly at the sound of that. Ulric continued, "Another thing that I have done for you on this island is that you will not age. You will always be the same in appearance, but you will grow in magical strength. You are destined to watch over and save this island in the future. No more questions for tonight. We will have plenty of time for questions later. Please, go get some rest because the morning will be here soon enough."

Karisma said, "Thank you?"

She turned back to the tower and made her way back to her new room. There was a comfortable bed near the window. The bed was more comfortable than any bed she had slept in. She laid down and did her best to get some sleep. There was too much information going through her mind to fall asleep. She tossed and turned, maybe falling asleep for a few minutes at the most.

Sunlight started to peek through the window. Karisma got up and peered out the window. The sun was just rising above the snow-capped mountains in the east. She excitedly sprinted down the stairs, out of the tower, and looked around. She saw that mountains surrounded the lake. The west shore of the lake, where the tower was located, had a soft and sandy shore. The sand was the type of sand which was perfect to build sandcastles on a sunny day at the beach. As the shoreline moved south, on the north and south sides, the sand turned into a rocky shoreline. The north side was very steep while the south side looked like the rock could be climbed over with some ease. She could not see the east shore from where she stood. The lake, from east to west, spread about a mile and half long. From north to south, the lake was a half mile in some spots and grew to three-quarters of a mile in others. The water was fresh and full of life. She watched fish jumping all over the lake. She saw some small crabs scurrying in and out of the water.

Karisma started to walk around and explore her new surroundings. Suddenly, out of nowhere, a dark-blue mist calmly floated toward her. The mist falling was like watching a leaf fall on an autumn day. The mist quickly changed into Ulric, who was holding a silver tray of breakfast for Karisma.

"Are you enjoying your lake?" asked Ulric.

"Yes, it is very beautiful and amazing. Thank you for the lovely meal," Karisma answered, still trying to absorb all the changes from the previous day.

Karisma and Ulric enjoyed a meal of fresh eggs that were from Ulric's chickens and some fresh rabbit meat.

Ulric said, "Just like I explained briefly last night, you *will* learn how to use magic. You will learn to use the magic, but you must never use this magic for evil or greed. This island, which I created, is for you to watch over. You were created, like I was many, many years ago, to keep learning and keep the magic of the wolf. My end is near, and you will be the last of the great wizards." Karisma looked at Ulric with some fear building in her eyes. "I will teach you," he reassured her. "You will also never be able to leave the island. I have bound you here to keep the magic safe. In turn, you will never age. There is a prophecy that I built into the creation of the island. You will learn this prophecy as I teach you the magic. You will learn that the prophecy is true, but how it unfolds is up to you. Do you have any questions for me?"

"I have lots, but I don't know how to ask them. When I am ready, I will let you know when I do. I just want to take all this in. Will I learn the mist thing? I guess I did have a question." Karisma giggled with a smile.

Ulric, smiling back, answered, "You will learn that in time and more."

CHAPTER 5

A Place of Learning

Early in the afternoon, Ulric took Karisma to his hut, which was in the middle of the island. To get to the hut, Ulric changed into a dragon, and Karisma rode on his back. He flew high enough so Karisma could see the entire island. She was amazed how different each region of the island was. The dense forest in the north to the fertile plains in the west to the mountains in the east—each region was very different and played a major role in how the island would prosper.

"What do you think of my island masterpiece?" asked Ulric.

"It is perfect. It might be the most beautiful place in the world," Karisma excitedly answered with a giant smile.

As she said this, Ulric suddenly rolled over and dove straight down to a loud and fearful scream from Karisma's mouth. He made the gentlest landing at the front of his hut. Ulric changed back to his human form.

The hut was maybe as old as Ulric, which was pretty amazing since the island was only created a few days ago. It was made of stacked logs and had a mix of straw and palm leaves as the roof. It had one door in the front and one open window next to the door. The hut was about ten feet by ten feet. Inside was plain. It had an old wooden bed with a mattress of straw. There was a fireplace in the corner and a table with two chairs near the fireplace.

"Welcome to my hut. We are now at the very center of the island. All the magic originates from here. This is sacred ground and must remain that way," Ulric cautiously advised. "There will be troubles coming to the island. It is up to you to keep the balance of peace and unity."

"I do not understand what you mean," Karisma replied.

Ulric answered, "You will understand in time. First, you must learn some basic magic."

The rest of the day went very quickly and was spent with Ulric teaching Karisma basic magic. Karisma, not only beautiful, was very smart. She learned everything quickly, which was a pleasant surprise to Ulric.

As the sun set, Ulric flew Karisma back to the tower.

"This tower is a place of security for you, a safe haven. You can leave at any time, but when you are here, you will be protected," Ulric said.

Karisma was only half listening because she was lost in the colors of the sunset. The sky was overflowing with a mix of reds, oranges, and purples, all changing into a star-filled nighttime canopy. She never knew there were so many stars in the sky.

The next day started just like the other. Breakfast was brought by Ulric, followed by a ride to the hut. This time Ulric flew west over the mountains and flew around the coast of the island. The west side of the island was steep cliffs that dropped straight into the ocean. The north side was picturesque, sandy beaches that changed quickly into the forest. The east side beaches turned slowly into the plains. Karisma was expecting the sudden descent to the hut, but this time Ulric glided softly to the ground.

Ulric began by saying, "The peace and unity of the island will be broken for a period of time, but you will restore the island so it will embrace peace and unity once again."

"How will I do that?" questioned Karisma.

"You will know what to do when the time comes," Ulric said, seeming unwilling to share something with Karisma.

She felt confused with the answer but just accepted that she would get an answer eventually.

"You said yesterday that I could never leave the island. What happens if I do?" Karisma asked.

"You will die. The world cannot handle a person of your beauty. You cannot leave, but in return, you will not age," Ulric bluntly reiterated with a sincere and comforting voice.

"Understood," said Karisma, confused and still trying to figure out what was going on.

Ulric replied, "You have a great responsibility on the island. Eventually, people will arrive here. You must determine their cause. Are they here for peace? Are they here for personal gain? You must decide. The balance and survival of the magic on the island is in your hands. I will teach you all that I know, but the choice is yours."

Weeks went by. Ulric continued to teach Karisma the magic of the wolf tribe. Karisma was now able to change forms. First, she mastered the blue mist, something that made her extremely happy. Then she was able to master changing into objects. Her personal favorite was to change into what she called the lake monster. It resembled a wingless dragon, with flippers on its feet, like a dolphin. It had a long neck, a long, skinny tail, and a head much like the one you would see on a dragon. Of course, Karisma made the monster able to breathe fire because fire was fun. This came in handy when it was time to start a campfire so she could warm up. She loved the lake monster because she was able to swim around the lake. The water was perfect for swimming. She could meditate on her thoughts in the peaceful serenity of the lake. She would think of her family and often wonder about how their kingdom was managing. She wondered if Az Rex would be able to hold to the standards of Ulric and become king.

CHAPTER 6

A Quest Begins

Back in Karisma's home kingdom, life went on normally. The king and queen remained with no memories of Karisma. Az Rex, however, kept having visions of a girl with long, dark hair and midnight-blue eyes. He had trouble sleeping because of these visions. One dark and dreary night, he decided to go through his childhood items. There he found his small swords. He remembered fighting the large knights with them, and he smiled at those thoughts. He kept on digging through his items and found pictures he had drawn. Each picture he drew of his family contained him, the king, the queen, and a girl with dark hair and dark-blue eyes. *Who is this girl?* he thought to himself, *I must find out. Why do I keep seeing her?*

The next day came, and Az Rex asked the queen about the girl in his pictures.

The queen answered with a puzzled look on her face, "I have never seen a girl with us. Did you make her up? Was she an imaginary girlfriend?"

Az Rex blushed and answered, "No, Mother. Every picture I had drawn of the family contains this girl. I keep seeing her in visions. I do not know if she needs help or if she is someone that I should know. Would she be a person from my childhood?"

The king walked into the room and looked at the pictures.

"Is this the person that you have chosen to be your wife?" the king asked.

"I do not know who she is, but I want to find out. Do you know who she might be?" Az Rex questioned his father.

"No, I do not." He cleared his throat. "I overheard you say that are having visions of her. You need to grow up and stop fantasizing about such nonsense. It is time you learned to rule the kingdom with an iron fist," scolded the king. "I shall call the kingdom's doctor at once. He can make you a serum that will make you forget these visions."

Az Rex bolted out of the castle the moment his father mentioned the doctor. He jumped on his horse and rode east, to the coastline. He knew there were some old caves that he could hide in, the same cave that he would travel to on childhood vacations. The ride took him a little over an hour. When he arrived, he entered one of the smaller caves; a piece of paper was crumbled up in the rocks on the ground. He picked up the paper and looked at it. It appeared to look like a map of an island. In the top left corner was an image of a wolf. In the bottom-right corner was an image of a flower petal. The map showed the location of a tower near a lake on the island. As he looked at the map, the island changed into a picture of a girl with long, dark hair.

"Is this part of my visions? What is this? Why is this happening to me?" he said, screaming out loud.

Az Rex spent the next week at the cave. He spent a lot of time meditating on what the visions meant. He grew restless and eventually came to the conclusion that he must know the girl and that they spent a lot of time together. In his mind, there could be no other explanation. He reasoned that she was in all his pictures that he drew as a child. Also, there were some drawings that he did as a child on the walls of the cave. She was also in those pictures as well.

"Is she in trouble? Does she need my help? Was she an old friend that I cannot remember?" were all questions that Az Rex wrestled with while he stayed in the cave.

His last night at the cave, a vision came to him in his dream. It was the girl. She was locked in a tower. The tower seemed to be guarded by some kind of lake monster. *She needs my help, and I will help her. Maybe she will become my wife after I rescue her. That will make my father proud that his kingdom will become mine, and I will have a wife to rule with,* he thought as he drifted into a deep sleep.

Az Rex dreamed of rescuing a girl in distress that night. His mind wondered how he could do that. Could he find the island on the map? The map looked like it was in uncharted waters. Was the map even real? Anyone could have drawn a map and placed it in a cave. Pirates hid their treasures, and maybe he could increase the wealth of the kingdom. What did the wolf and flower petal mean? Why did this girl keep coming to him? Was she real? What was her name? All these questions raced through his mind as he tried to sleep.

The next morning Az Rex rode back to the castle. He snuck around to the back to avoid his parents. He did not want to see the doctor and drink a potion that would make him forget something that he sensed was very real. He made his way to the back of the castle, to the hallway where the knights had their rooms. He found one of the knights, the one that was known as Oton the Fierce. He was tall, close to seven feet tall when his armor was on. The armor was made of the purest silver, a high honor for all the accomplishments he had done for the king. His sword was a marvelous wonder. The handle was made a white gold. The blade was made mostly of gold, and the center of the blade was made of silver. When he took off the armor, he was a tall man, standing around six and a half feet. His black hair was short and curly. He had a short beard and a long mustache. His eyes squinted in the light. His skin was pale, but that was from being in the armor most of the time. He was very trusted by the king and queen. In fact, Oton the Fierce was the same knight that the king sent on the quest for the flower many years earlier.

Az Rex asked a simple question, "Can you go on a quest for the king and queen?" Az Rex knew that Oton the Fierce would never deny going on a quest.

"What quest is this?" Oton the Fierce had a thunderously deep voice and replied with great excitement. "Please let me know."

Az Rex handed the map to Oton the Fierce and said, "We need to find this mysterious island. Something important is there, and we need to find out what it is. To me, it looks like a tower. I want to know who lives in this tower."

"I will leave as soon as I gather my crew and the ship is ready to set sail," Oton the Fierce said with a giant-sized smile that went from ear to ear.

"Report back to me when you find this island. I do not want to bother my father and mother with these small and trivial things," Az Rex said.

A few hours later, Oton the Fierce assembled his crew, finished packing the ship, and set sail on his journey. Oton the Fierce was regarded in the kingdom as the best sailor in the world. He could make any trip faster than any other sailor, and he also had the unique ability to find anything. Combining these two skills together, Az Rex felt very hopeful that the mysterious island and girl would be found.

Oton the Fierce, in his many quests and journeys, had heard tales of an uncharted island about a day and a half to the east. He decided that was where his journey should begin. He was also sure that he would be there in a day because he was the best sailor in the world.

The trip east was uneventful. The crew spent most of the day scrubbing the ship and keeping busy. There was some downtime that was spent practicing sword-fighting. Oton the Fierce was also the greatest swordsman in the kingdom, and no one could come close to beating him. He would humor the men by fighting them, just for entertainment's sake.

As the day turned into night, a violent storm came up and over-took them. The waves grew to unnatural heights, which had never been seen before. A heavy rain grew and washed some of the crew overboard. It was the most vicious storm that Oton the Fierce had ever seen. The lightning was bright and endless. The thunder rocked the boat. One of the bolts of lightning seemed to take the shape of a wolf. Many years later, as the story was passed on, it was assumed that the crew was drunk with rum and seeing visions in the sky.

As the sun rose in the east, the storm just vanished as quickly as it started. "Land hoe!" was yelled from a storm-battered crewman in the crow's nest. Oton the Fierce's plan was to sail around the island

and take notes and then compare the notes to the map that Az Rex had given him. The trip around the island took the full amount of daylight. The crew spent the night making repairs from the previous night's storm.

While the crew was hard at work, making repairs, Oton the Fierce looked at his notes and the map and believed that this was the island that Az Rex wanted to find. Oton the Fierce decided the only way to truly tell was to explore the island by foot. The map showed a lake and tower on the northern coast of the lake. The next morning, Oton the Fierce and ten members of his crew jumped into a lifeboat and rowed toward the western shore.

The shore was made of soft and powdery white sand, which stuck to everyone's feet as they got off the lifeboat. The beach was only about one hundred yards long, then the landscape changed into wide open fields. The fields were covered with grasses and flowers of all kinds. It was hard to tell how far the fields went, but mountains could be seen off in the distance. Oton the Fierce knew by looking at the map that the landing party needed to get to those mountains. That was where the tower was located. The faster they got there, the faster they could bring the news back to Az Rex.

The crew was walking through the fields when someone cried out, "Dragon!"

Everyone ducked for cover in the tall grass while Oton the Fierce grabbed for his bow to fire an arrow at the vicious-looking beast. Before Oton the Fierce could load the arrow, the dragon disappeared in the sky. One of the crewmen swore to the day he died that the dragon just disappeared into a blue mist. Oton the Fierce and the rest of the crew never believed that story, thinking the dragon was just too fast for them to shoot with an arrow. Oton the Fierce gave the men the orders from that moment forward to be ready with their weapons at all times.

They finally reached the end of the fertile fields, which ended at a river. The river slowly and lazily flowed to the south. The river was about twenty yards across, and the other side was a forest that separated the fields from the mountains. The water was clear as fine crystal glasses that the king and queen used at the palace and was full of fish.

Oton the Fierce decided that they should take a break from their journey here. He sat on a medium-sized rock and rested while his crew did their work. One of the crewmen caught some fish while a second crewman started a fire to cook the fish. While the fish was cooking, Oton the Fierce looked across the river. He saw a very dense forest that started to climb into the mountains. *This is going to be slow travel through the forest,* he thought to himself, because there were no paths, and they would have to cut their way through the trees and branches. Oton the Fierce took a second look at the forest just as a wolf ran through the trees. The wolf stopped long enough to glare at Oton the Fierce. The wolf's fur had a blue tint to it. Oton the Fierce thought it was because of the shadows in the forest.

After all the crew ate and were satisfied, the hike continued. They knew they had to cross the river, but they had a problem with that. Oton the Fierce could not swim because of the weight of his armor, and he did not want to leave it behind. The order given by Oton the Fierce was to have the whole crew had to look for another way to cross. About a mile down the stream, the crew found a large tree that had fallen across a narrower part of the river. The tree was cedar, a strong wood, and Oton the Fierce knew it would hold his weight. Oton the Fierce crossed first and each crew member followed, one by one. As they entered the forest, a thunderous howling sound was heard from deep within the forest. Oton the Fierce squeezed his sword and was ready for action at any moment as the crew made their way into the forest toward the mountains.

The sun started to set, and the group gathered some dry wood to make a fire for the night. It was decided that each member of the group would take a two-hour watch, pairing up, just in case something was lurking in the woods. The group had already encountered a dragon and a wolf, and Oton the Fierce did not want to be taken by surprise on an unknown island. The bright and giant full moon rose, and Oton the Fierce and his crew took turns sleeping for the night.

The night was uneventful. Morning came, and everyone woke up, ate a quick breakfast of nuts and berries, and then started the journey toward the mountains. The forest was relentless and exhausting but eventually opened to a clearing. As the group entered the small clearing, the wolf ran in front of them. Oton the Fierce threw his sword at the wolf, but the wolf just disappeared.

"We must have found the wolves' den," Oton the Fierce bravely said to the crew.

He appointed two men to go explore what was believed to be the den. When the men arrived where the sword landed, nothing was found. The men reported what they had seen back to Oton the Fierce. He was extremely frustrated with the report about the den, but not wanting to waste any more time, the group continued the day's journey.

A spring of bubbling water was in the south part of the clearing. The men drank some of the water to get ready for the trip into the mountains. As they drank, strange but magical things started to happen. One of the men, who was a bit slower compared to the rest of the crew due to being sick that morning, was suddenly cured. Another one of the men swore that he could see to the top of the mountains. He described everything in detail that was on the peak, but Oton the Fierce did not believe his story.

"Enough of this nonsense. You all need to get your minds back on course. Let us now head north to the mountain pass," Oton the Fierce sternly commanded to the crew.

The group picked up their pace and made fast time through the clearing and arrived at the mountain pass. The pass looked like it could be traveled through with ease. From what Oton the Fierce could gather from the map, the lake should be located on the other side of the pass. A dragon could be seen flying through the pass. Oton the Fierce wasn't worried about a dragon because of his strength. Oton the Fierce, from the time he was a small child, was taught not to fear anything and have absolute faith in his ability and equipment. His armor was built to be fireproof, and the kingdom's magician made a spell to ensure it. He was losing patience at the monotony of traveling. He just wanted to find the lake and make the report back to Az Rex.

The mountain pass was beautiful. Trees sprouted up against the rocks. The peaks were snow-covered, but the pass was between the peaks, so the snow would not be a problem. It wasn't steep, but it was still uphill. Anything uphill in armor was not fun, but it had to be done.

The climb up the start of the pass was easy. The group made good time. As the group reached the top of the pass, Oton the Fierce noticed some gold nuggets scattered about the ground. *Maybe I should keep this island a secret and keep the gold,* he schemed to himself. He would be rich and rule this island. He would not be "just a knight" to anyone anymore. Just as his thought finished, a giant fireball flew through the air toward the group, engulfing one of the men. The man turned to dust instantly, and as his body turned to ash, a gold nugget fell from what used to be his hand.

"Don't touch the gold," commanded Oton the Fierce to the nine remaining crewmen. "The dragon is protecting the gold. Keep your arms at the ready, and be ready for anything."

The group made their way to the north side of the pass. The pass opened into a steep valley. Oton the Fierce looked down toward the valley, and all he could see were lots of trees. He could not tell how far the valley dropped toward the ground, but he knew the lake and tower were down there. Oton the Fierce led the group down the pass into the dense forest. The travel was painfully slow. After what seemed like days, he could smell fresh water in the air. The forest grew less dense with each step. The forest ended and a rocky shoreline was in view.

"I found it! I found the missing lake. I shall name it Oton Lake, in memory of our journey here," Oton the Fierce exclaimed.

The rocky shore emptied into a beautiful lake. The water was midnight blue in color and had small rippling waves that lapped gently on the rocks. The dragon landed off in the distance, staring at the group.

CHAPTER 7

Encounter at the Lake

Karisma had spent the last few days in her tower practicing all the new magic she had learned when Ulric joined her in her room. He informed her of the group of, as he put it, "unwanted visitors" that had been exploring the island. He told her how he had been following them as a wolf and a dragon, being attacked anytime he came close to them. Ulric also explained that one man was killed because he was trying to steal things from the island.

"The leader is a knight from your parent's kingdom, sent by your brother. You need to find out what they are up to and how they found out about this island," Ulric said before he suddenly disappeared.

Karisma noticed that Ulric had a worried look in his eyes.

Karisma looked out her window and saw some smoke in the distance. It looked like a campfire, but she wanted to see for herself. Karisma dove out the window into a double front flip and, with the help of magic, cleared the sixty feet between the tower and the lake. She landed with a giant splash in the water and changed into her lake monster. Karisma sped to the east end of the lake, where the smoke seemed to be coming from. She got within a hundred feet of the shore before she could see the group of men standing around the campfire, talking among themselves. Karisma stuck her head out of the water, trying to hear what they were saying, but she was too far away. She quietly swam toward the coastline, trying to get within an earshot of the group. One of the men happened to look at the lake and yelled, "Monster!" when he saw Karisma's head poking out of the water. The whole group turned in unison and grabbed their weapons.

"This ugly beast of a monster is guarding the tower!" exclaimed Oton the Fierce. "We must slay the beast." He shot his arrows toward Karisma. The rest of the men followed his actions, shooting arrows at the lake.

Karisma quickly dove to the bottom of the lake. *I will be safe here*, she thought. *What are they up to? Why did they attack me?* were questions she asked herself. Karisma slowly started to make her way back to the tower, but she was stopped by Ulric, who was waiting for her under the water. Karisma was surprised to see Ulric under the water, but at the same time, she was not surprised anymore.

"They *must not be allowed* to make it to the tower. I have taught you before, that is a place of sacred magic. It is a place that only a select few are allowed to enter, ones that are worthy and have a true heart. None of *them* have been found worthy to enter," Ulric continued to teach Karisma.

"Who is worthy to enter? What is a true heart? What does all this mean?" Karisma frustratingly asked.

"There will be only *one other* that will be found worthy to enter the tower. Her heart will be true and pure. Many years from now, she will come to unite the island to what it is now, a place of magic and unity. The one will have the hair of gold and eyes of the sky," answered Ulric, once again using one of his riddles.

"When will this take place?" Karisma answered with a question.

"Two generations will pass before the only one worthy will be born," Ulric continued. "Four generations will pass before the worthy one will start her quest to bring the island back together into one."

Karisma, looking puzzled, questioned, "What does that mean? Why then? Why her? Why is she so special? Is the island going to break apart?"

Ulric slyly answered back, "All of this will be revealed to you in time." After he said that, he disappeared as quickly as he appeared.

Karisma, now confused, restarted her swim back to the tower with even more thoughts flowing through her mind. *Ulric is very secretive*, she thought as she reached the tower.

Oton the Fierce gathered his men and started a fast march to the west side of the lake. "The beast must be killed. It has to be protecting something in the tower, and *I will* find out what," he said to his men.

Karisma stared out the window as the sun started to set, watching the group of men come closer and closer to the tower. For the first time in her life, she felt fear building inside of her. Oton the Fierce looked toward the tower and saw Karisma standing in the window. The two made eye contact.

"There is a beautiful lady in the tower. That is why the dragon tried to kill us. We must rescue her from the lake monster. Az Rex will be happy with this find," Oton the Fierce commanded. Some of the men started wading in the water, trying to stir the monster. "You, watch the tower. I will go slay the monster and claim the prize for Prince Az Rex," Oton was heard saying as he ran toward the water.

"They are going to destroy the peacefulness of this island," Karisma cried as she watched the men, with sword drawn and bow at the ready, surround the tower.

Karisma vanished from the tower and reappeared in the lake, changing to the lake monster. She bravely swam to the shore, where the men were waiting for a battle. Karisma wanted to make them understand that the island was a place of peace and unity, not war or battles.

As Karisma was making her way to the shoreline, Oton the Fierce made his way to the tower door. He tried to open the large wooden door, but it was locked—not with a lock but with magic. He could not break it with his body. Oton the Fierce used his sword to bash the door down, but nothing happened until his once mighty sword broke into two pieces. *The lady in the tower is in a lot of trouble. No one would seal the door like this unless there was trouble*, Oton the Fierce thought to himself. He began to look around for another way into the tower.

Karisma reached the shoreline as Oton the Fierce's sword broke.

One of the men yelled, "*Monster!*"

Karisma was both saddened and scared that the men were afraid of her. She never made a quick movement to scare them, and she never attacked any of the men. She just wanted to talk to them. One of the men shot his arrows at her. The arrows bounced off her scales and fell into the lake. Another of the men ran toward her with his sword ready to strike.

Finally, Karisma got the courage to speak.

"Don't attack, this is a peaceful place," she pleaded with the men.

"Don't listen to the monster. Kill it," shouted one of the men in a loud voice, ignoring the fact that a lake monster just spoke to them.

Oton the Fierce heard all the commotion coming from the lake and ran toward the shore. He grabbed a sword from one of his men and was ready to fight. Karisma turned her head and saw Oton the Fierce rushing at full speed toward where she was. She shot out a ball of fire from her mouth. Oton the Fierce was stopped in his tracks when the fireball hit him in the middle of his body. His armor fell, and his body turned to ashes, blowing in the small breeze.

The men saw Oton the Fierce fall.

One of them yelled, "Kill the monster! Now! Avenge the death of Oton the Fierce!"

The men ran at Karisma to attack her. She dove into the water and sprung up in another spot. There she shot another fireball, burning all except three of the men that traveled in the group. Armor and ashes littered the once peaceful shoreline.

CHAPTER 8

Reporting Back to Az Rex

The three surviving men left Kingsbridge Lake, not Oton Lake, quickly. The men sprinted toward the valley. It was getting dark, but they did not care. The men made their way up the valley and down the pass in the dark. They wanted to get back to the ship as quickly as they could. The dense forest made travel extremely hard, and it took the entire next day to make it to the river where they decided to spend the night.

The next morning the men awoke to birds singing. They ate some nuts they found and ran to the fields just ahead of them, not looking back at the mountains. They saw the rowboat just ahead of them. Once they reached it, they jumped in the boat and fearfully rowed back to the ship, hoping there was not a monster in the water. There they gave the grave news about the death of Oton the Fierce and the rest of the crew. With saddened hearts, the crew sailed back to give the news to Az Rex.

The ship entered the harbor just after sundown and was greeted by Az Rex himself. They gave the news of all the events of that happened in great detail. Az Rex reacted with great anger toward the monster. He wanted to get revenge. He also felt a lust for the mysterious and beautiful woman that the men described; he wanted her as his wife, and there was no doubt that she was the lady in his visions.

There will be no stopping me on both of these quests. I am stronger than Oton the Fierce, and I will not fail, thought Az Rex.

Az Rex stormed back to his parents' castle and started to make preparations to go to the mysterious island.

The king saw Az Rex in the middle of his secret work and calmly questioned, "What are you doing, Az Rex?"

Az Rex answered, "I am making preparations to go slay a monster and rescue a beautiful woman in distress. She is in a tower that is guarded by a lake monster."

Confused, the king asked, "Where is this monster and woman?"

"It is on an island, about a day's trip from here. Oton the Fierce mapped the island's location," answered Az Rex.

"Where is Oton the Fierce now? I want to question him about this island,." the king probed.

Az Rex quietly answered, "He is dead. He was slain by a lake monster."

Surprised and angered by the news, the king backhanded Az Rex across his right cheek and yelled angrily, "What do you mean Oton the Fierce is dead? Did you send my greatest knight to an unknown island without my permission? If a commoner did this, I would have to hold court to judge him. Should you face the same punishment for your crime against the crown? Stay in your room, and I will deal with you tomorrow. Maybe I will spare your life."

Az Rex, with anger building in eyes, grabbed his sword and stuck his father in the chest. Az Rex, now filled with great fear, ran from the castle to the harbor.

"What have I done to my father? I need to leave this place now to save my own life," he said as he ran swiftly.

The queen walked down the hall by Az Rex's room and was surprised when she saw the king clutching his chest, lying in a pool of blood.

"*Guards!* Come quickly," she screamed. "Who would have done this to my husband?"

"Az Rex," softly answered the king, coughing and clinging to life.

The queen had some of the guards take the king to his bed-chamber. The other guards searched for Az Rex. She also had the doctor summoned immediately to the chambers for the emergency. The doctor of the kingdom rushed in just as the king was brought into the room and carefully laid on the bed.

"There is nothing that I can do. The wound is deep, but I can prolong his life through the night with some surgery and serums. The king *will* die before the sun rises tomorrow morning. There is nothing that I do to stop that," the doctor explained to the queen.

The queen sat next to the king and wept out loud. The doctor left the room. The guards stood in disbelief. Suddenly a blue mist appeared in the middle of the room. The mist changed into an old man.

"Do you remember me?" the old man quizzed the queen.

"No. Should I?" the queen answered. "Why are you here? Can you not see that I am weeping for my husband, the king?"

The old man slammed his staff on the ground. A thunderous sound happened when the staff hit the ground, and the king's and queen's memories suddenly returned to them.

"Ulric?" said the queen. "The old wizard that gave us twins?"

"It is I," answered Ulric.

"You took my beautiful daughter away. I should have you killed on the spot, but why do you come to us now?" the queen questioned. "Can you save my husband?"

Ulric answered, "No, I cannot, and I will not, but that is not why I am here. Az Rex will not rule the kingdom."

"But you promised we would have an heir to the throne forever," interrupted the queen.

"I never said *what* kingdom would be ruled by your offspring. I also never said which of your children would rule," answered Ulric. "The end of your husband's rule is coming to an end. Hide the triplets. By the sunset tomorrow, this kingdom will stand no more. This is the judgment handed to you and your kingdom for the countless number of wars. Az Rex's heart will grow with anger, just like his father's. That anger will be the end of him."

The king looked at Ulric and tried to answer, but all that was heard was him choking on his own blood.

The queen answered, "Understood. I will do as you wish. Tell Karisma that we are sorry and that we will always love her."

After she said this, Ulric vanished. A moment after Ulric vanished, the king took his final breath before the doctor could start his procedure.

The queen took a quick moment to bow her head toward her husband, and then she ran toward the boys' room. She ordered the guards to take them away from the castle, never to return.

"Keep them hidden. There is a city south of here in the desert. Find someone to take care of them, and I pray that they will be safe," the queen commanded.

The three guards took the triplets away immediately. The six of them made their way to the small city to the south. The city was old and not part of the kingdom. It was a place that no one would recognize any of them.

The next morning, a rival and brutal kingdom stormed the castle. The attackers left no survivors, including the queen. Az Rex's kingdom was gone, forever to be forgotten.

Az Rex boarded a ship to sail to the new island, not knowing that his kingdom had fallen in the attack. The first half day, the trip went extremely smooth, but a monstrous storm came up and blew the ship off course. Az Rex and his crew were lost and stranded in the middle of the ocean. Their ship was stuck, and there was nothing Az Rex could do about it. A couple of years went by, and Az Rex grew in anger.

CHAPTER 9

The Storm at Sea

The story of a woman in a tower on the island spread around all the countries of the world. Many knights would make the once impossible to trip to the island with great ease. They all wanted two things. The first was to slay the horrible lake monster. The second was to take the woman in the tower as their wife. Karisma grew frustrated at the knights and their quests for violence.

Karisma decided to make a visit to Ulric to ask questions. She wanted some answers. When she arrived at Ulric's hut, she found it empty, and the door was wide open.

"Ulric? Where are you? I have many questions for you," she said.

She entered the hut and looked around. There was an old and tattered map lying on a table. The map had a written note saying, "Az Rex." The name pointed to a location in the middle of the ocean.

"Did you find anything of interest?" questioned Ulric as he quietly entered the hut and startled Karisma.

Karisma, regaining her composure, asked, "What is this map with my brother's name?"

"He had to be stopped. He was on his way here, for revenge. That is something that will not be tolerated on this island," replied Ulric.

Karisma interrupted, "Did you kill him?"

"No, he is not dead. He is lost at sea. I will give him and his crew what is needed to survive. The map is magical and will always show his current location as the ship just floats in the middle of the ocean," Ulric answered.

Karisma, trying to outsmart her teacher, asked, "Revenge for what? He did not do anything on the island."

"His revenge was for the deaths he caused by sending Oton the Fierce to this island to explore the first time. His revenge is for the death of your father, caused by his own sword. His revenge is internal, something he has to do in his own mind. Nothing will stop him," Ulric tried to explain.

"Where have you been?" Karisma cautiously questioned with a look of distrust in her eyes.

Ulric answered, "I had to put a stop to the killings and greed in your old kingdom."

"What does that mean?" a tearful Karisma questioned.

Ulric, being as truthful as he could, answered with a great gentleness, "When the news of Oton the Fierce's death reached your brother, Az Rex swore revenge on the *monster* that killed him. Az Rex also lusted over the woman in the tower. He will not stop until he gets both things he wants. You father confronted Az Rex about the journey he was about to embark on. During the confrontation, Az Rex struck your father with a lethal slash to the heart." Karisma's eyes swelled with tears when she heard this news, hoping what she heard the moment before was a misunderstanding. "As punishment for the war and for the greed, the kingdom fell and is no more. The kingdom will be long forgotten and hidden in history."

Karisma interrupted, "What about my other brothers, the ones I left when they were one?"

Ulric continued, "They are safe. The three most trusted guards took them to a faraway southern city. They will be raised by commoners there. No one in the city will learn their true identities, as princes."

"This is a lot to take in," answered Karisma with tears falling down her cheeks.

Ulric wiped away her tears and said with the excitement of a good teacher, "You have done as I taught you. You kept the island safe. You kept the tower safe. People will continue to come. The legend of the monster has already spread around the world. Eventually, the legend will stop, but for now, your job is to protect the magic of this island. There will be a time that this island will inhabit people, but now is not that time. You need to go back to your tower because you have a lot on your mind. Get some rest, and your mother told me to tell you one last thing, that she will always love you."

Ulric waved his hand, and Karisma vanished to her room in the tower.

Tears fell down Karisma's cheeks as she looked out the window. Through the pain and confusion, she was calmed by the peace and beauty of the lake. The sun was just starting to set, making a brilliant color of orange in the sky that reflected off the lake. The slow-moving ripples made such a soft and serene sound it put her into a deep sleep.

She slept until the next afternoon. She awoke to the sound of birds squawking near the shore. Karisma looked and saw some large blue jays and watched as they fought over some blueberries in the bushes. Karisma laughed at the sight of this.

"Just like people, they always want more," she said.

Karisma washed her face, brushed her hair, changed into clean clothes, and decided to go for a walk on the shore. The south shore was littered with armor, weapons, and ashes. As she made her way east, the shore became clean. The beach was full of soft sand and beautiful forest started at the edge of the sand. Karisma found a rock and sat on the sand, with her back against the rock, and started to think. *I can save Az Rex and help him understand that revenge is not needed. He is my brother. He will listen to me. We were best friends growing up. I need to find a way to reach him.* Karisma stared off into the bright-blue sky, watching the high-flying, white, fluffy clouds. Hours passed, but it only seemed to be a few minutes. Karisma finally came up with an idea. She created an image of herself in a cloud and sent the cloud to Az Rex. The cloud drifted ever so softly to the south, over the mountains, and out of sight.

Az Rex and his crew were busy trying to figure out where they were and how to get moving so he could get to the elusive island. He looked up from his work and saw a cloud floating toward him. The cloud had the shape of a woman.

As the cloud approached, it started speaking, "Az Rex, do not fear me. I am your twin sister, Karisma. Give up your lust for revenge, turn around, and head for a safe harbor in another kingdom. Our kingdom is gone, gone forever. Start a new life for yourself. Be free from your lust and be free from fear."

Az Rex, stricken with a terrorizing fear, grabbed his sword and slashed at the cloud. The cloud split in two and the reshaped back into one.

"I am seeing things. The years of wasted time is playing tricks on me. This storm is playing with my mind."

The misty cloud answered, "You are not seeing things in your mind. What you see is real. I am using magic, which I have learned to send you this message. Please listen to my plea, I beg you. The path you choose now will only lead to your death. Change your path and save yourself."

Az Rex interrupted, "Away from me, demon. The spirits are playing tricks on me for killing my father. I will have my revenge and take my prize of the woman in the tower. Nothing will stop me, not even the spirit of my dead father. His kingdom will be mine."

As Karisma heard Az Rex, she started to cry. As she cried, the cloud turned into a giant, raging storm. The waves grew to over forty feet tall and washed more than half the crew overboard. The storm raged on for the next ten days. Az Rex and his crew somehow kept the ship from going down, but many repairs were needed to stay afloat.

Ulric once again appeared to Karisma when she was in her tower and asked, "Do you have any news for me?"

Karisma looked tearfully at Ulric. Knowing she could not hide anything from him, she told Ulric the whole story.

Ulric angrily replied, "Do you now understand why Az Rex has to be stopped? His lust for revenge has consumed all of his thoughts. He is sick, and there is no cure for his lust. Leaving him to live out his days on a ship in the middle of the ocean was the best plan, but your interference caused a different outcome to the solution."

"I understand now. I am sorry for making things more of a mess," answered a sorrowful Karisma. "This storm needs to stop, and I am the one to make it stop."

Ulric replied, "That is in your control. First, you must learn how to control your emotions. Once you learn this, then you will be able to stop the storm."

CHAPTER 10

Meeting at the Hut

Ulric left Karisma alone in her tower, and she thought about what he said. She started to think of all the good things she had on the island, all the birds and animals the mountains and streams and the beauty of the island. She thought about how she saved the island from Oton the Fierce and his men and how she also stopped all the other knights that came and wanted to save a princess for their own glory. She smiled and her heartfelt a peace that she had never felt before. As her heart filled with this peace, the storm started to lift. The sun peeked through the clouds and shone all over the island. The birds around the lake started to sing loudly as the water stopped dripping from the trees. Karisma smiled as she felt the joy the island brought to her.

Ulric appeared in Karisma's room.

"I have news," he said. "My time is soon coming to an end. When I am gone, the island will be yours. Remember, you control the destiny of the island. There will be a time coming soon that the magic will fail, but one will come that will restore the magic. You will teach her, in the same way I taught you, and the island will be restored to its glory once again."

Karisma interrupted Ulric, "Where are you going? Why are you leaving? What time has ended?"

Ulric teared up and calmly replied, "I will be gone forever. A foe will be here soon, one that is overcome with the lust for power. I cannot stop him. That is up to you, my greatest creation."

"Az Rex," said Karisma with a look of shame and sadness on her face.

"I must go and prepare for what is to come to me. Rest here. You will need to be ready for what is to come," Ulric said as he disappeared and left Karisma's tower for what would be the final time.

Az Rex finally regained control of his ship after the storm stopped.

"Land hoe!" was announced from the bow of the ship.

Az Rex commanded, "The storm blew us to an island. Sail around this island. This might be the place we have been looking for."

"Aye, aye, sir," came from one of the crewmen.

The ship slowly limped its way around the island. Az Rex kept looking at his map and also looking at the notes that Oton the Fierce made on his last journey. Az Rex made mental notes so he did not have to pull the map out to look it at it over and over again. He found where Oton the Fierce landed his party. The mountains that Oton the Fierce noted the pass was in appeared as the ship made its way to the south shore.

"This is indeed the island that Oton the Fierce found for me. Prepare a flag. I will claim this island for myself when we reach the beach," said Az Rex. "This will make a great addition to my future kingdom. An addition that my father was too afraid to make."

The ship ran aground and the fifteen men that were left still alive got off the boat and gratefully touched and kissed the solid ground after a two-year voyage in the ocean. They walked like they had too much rum as they walked on a nonmoving ground. Az Rex planted his flag on the beach and made a small speech, which no one really listened to because it was all about him. The crew seemed unimpressed, but they had to submit to their leader. Looking at the map, Az Rex decided that he wanted to head to the center of the island first because the map was blank in the center of the island, and he wanted to see what was there. Some of the men reluctantly followed, and others refused. The men that refused were warned that their lives were at stake when Az Rex lifted his bloodstained sword, from the heart of his father, toward one of the men. After Az Rex's subtle persuasion, the crew followed him and started the journey to the center of the island.

Az Rex started by following the same path that Oton the Fierce followed in his journey. Eventually, Az Rex and his crew made their way through the grasses and weeds. His thoughts were set on ruling the island, finding the woman in his dreams, and being the one to explore the center of the island. The more he thought about the center of the island, the more he was angered about Oton the Fierce for not doing more exploring of the island. He would have less work to do and then take that credit from Oton the Fierce, the knight who lost to the lake monster. The more Az Rex thought about that, the less he thought about the "weak" knight.

After a few hours, Az Rex and his men found a river. After all the rain, the river was flowing quickly and swelled to the tops of its banks.

"We need to cross this river," Az Rex commanded the whole group. While looking at one of the men that resisted the journey earlier, he delegated, "You, prove your loyalty and swim across this river and secure the rope so we can all cross."

"Sir, the water is moving too fast for anyone to swim across," the man protested with fear.

Az Rex drew his sword and poked the tip of it into the man's chest and whispered, "You went against me once. *Do not* make the same mistake twice."

The man jumped in, and the current was so strong he was washed away within a few seconds, never to be seen again.

"He got what he deserved. Does anyone else want to defy my authority?" Az Rex boldly challenged his men. "Now, since I have your attention, let us make our way upriver and find a place to cross. We will need to find a place to camp for the night. The sun will set soon."

The group made their way west, following the river. They came to a place where the water was not as high and more spread out. It was only about knee high. Az Rex made his way to the middle of the river and commanded his men to follow him. Finally fed up with Az Rex's lust for power, six of the men turned around and were heading back to the ship. The remaining eight men stood at the bank, watching Az Rex.

"Come on, cross the river now!" Az Rex demanded.

One of the men raised his bow and took aim at Az Rex. Az Rex dove into the water to avoid the incoming arrow. Az Rex looked at the remaining men and ran at them with his sword ready.

A few minutes later, the eight men were left dead, and Az Rex was left fuming, "They will all die."

Az Rex decided to make his way across the river. He would deal with his rebellious traitors later. When he got to the middle of the river, he used the water to clean his sword. The red water flowed slowly with the current. Karisma, sitting in her tower, felt a saddening within the island.

Once Az Rex got to the other side of the river, he encountered a dark, dense forest. The walk through the forest was slower than the walk through the field. After a couple of hours, he found a small clearing and made camp for the night there. He found a medium-sized squirrel for his dinner that night. The fire was warm on the cool night. Az Rex drifted off to sleep for the night but also staying alert mentally just in case his crew came for him.

Dawn came, and the birds started to sing. Az Rex woke up, stretched his back, and continued his journey to the center of the island.

The walk was painfully slow. Az Rex kept checking the map and making judgments of where to go next. He felt like he was going in circles. Each tree looked the same, very large and very green. After a few more hours, Az Rex stumbled onto a large clearing.

In the center of the clearing was a small hut. The door was shut, and the window was covered. Az Rex looked around and saw no one in the area. From the distance, a wolf's howl was heard. Az Rex bashed the door in and looked around the one room hut. He looked at the small bed. Next to the bed, he noticed a creepy-looking walking cane. The wall across from the door had a fireplace. The fireplace looked well used but was cold.

"Az Rex, why are you here?" came from a voice behind Az Rex.

Az Rex quickly turned around and said, "Who dares address me? Show yourself to me."

"You need to leave this island. You will only find your doom," said the mysterious voice. This time it came from the fireplace.

Az Rex drew his sword, "Who are you?"

"I am Ulric, a great wizard of the wolf tribe," said the voice. "You do not know me, but I know you." Ulric slowly appeared, sitting on the bed, holding his cane.

"How would you know me? I have never met such an old man before," questioned a startled Az Rex.

"I created you and your twin sister, Karisma," Ulric explained. "Your parents begged me for children. You were made to be the heir to your parents' throne, but your lusts have taken that right away from you. You will have nothing."

"You are a liar. I have no sister. My lust for power is my greatest asset. Without that lust, I would not be able to expand my kingdom," Az Rex arrogantly said. "This pathetic island is the newest addition to my mighty kingdom."

"Your kingdom is gone. The palace is in ruin, and your parents are dead," Ulric scolded Az Rex.

Az Rex smiled and asked, "I killed my father?"

Ulric questioned, "You are happy that you did this?"

"He stood in my way. He did not want me to explore. He did not want me to follow my lusts for greatness. No one will ever stand in the way of my power ever again," answered Az Rex with a deranged smile upon his face. "Who had the special honor of killing my mother? I hope they enjoyed it."

Ulric answered, "It does not matter. The kingdom is gone."

"It does matter. I can use that in my revenge. I will also assume that my three-year-old brothers are dead as well. They could not take care of themselves at that age. I will regain the former glory of the kingdom when I get home after I take control of this pathetic island," Az Rex boldly claimed.

"You will not make it off this island alive," interrupted Ulric. "You will die here. There is no stopping that."

Az Rex reached for his sword and proclaimed, "Are you going to kill me, old man? Strike at me, and *you* will die."

"Not I but another on this island has the power to stop you," Ulric calmly said.

Az Rex's eyes turned red with anger as he said, "You are insane. The only other person on this island is a woman." He lifted his sword to Ulric's chest. "There is no way she, or any other woman, would be strong enough to stop me," said an angered Az Rex as he stabbed Ulric in his heart. "Say goodbye." Az Rex chuckled as he turned the sword to kill Ulric quickly.

Ulric's body vanished as he died. The island shook with a giant earthquake. A large wave came up and destroyed Az Rex's ship, leaving nothing of it. Everyone that deserted Az Rex vanished and was never to be seen again. Legend has it they appeared on Easter Island, but no one can confirm or deny that story. Az Rex, not fazed by any of the events that just transpired, exited the hut. As he left, he set fire to the hut, leaving it in ashes.

"No one will remember this place, the center of the island where an old insane hermit lived alone. Now off to claim my prize, the woman in the tower."

Az Rex quickly hurried on his way to find the tower by the lake.

CHAPTER 11

At the Lake

Many thoughts poured through Karisma's mind as she spent the night cleaning up the giant mess in her room from the earthquake from the previous night. She knew deep in her heart that Ulric had died and that his death caused the earthquake. She was also concerned for her brother. *How could he become so caught up in the lust for power that he would forget the kindness that he shared when they were children?* Karisma thought. After all, he did come to her rescue when they were younger. She knew in heart that it was her time to rescue him, but she had to keep her emotions from taking over like they did with the giant storm. It was time for her to use what she had learned.

After the room was cleaned and swept, Karisma decided that she should go to Ulric's hut. She wanted to check up on him, hoping her assumptions of his death were not true and that he would be waiting to teach her another lesson. Karisma appeared in the clearing, next to the still smoldering hut. Her heart sank as she saw the ashes. In the middle of the ashes was Ulric's burned staff. She fell on her knees and started to cry. Karisma now came to realize that her brother had to be stopped. She wanted to help him, but was that task impossible? She wondered where the brother of her childhood went. She needed some time to think about that question.

Karisma changed into a magnificent-looking dragon, with black scales, large wings, and midnight-blue eyes. Karisma took off and flew slowly over the island, searching for Az Rex. She spotted him running east, along the edge of the forest near the pass to the lake. She landed on the mountain pass and changed back to her human form. She was going to wait for Az Rex and try to talk to him, hoping that she could bring him back to his childhood memories.

Az Rex made his way to the pass and followed the rocky trail that was littered with gold. He hurried past the ashes on the ground of what used to be the member of Oton the Fierce's crew. As he ran forward, he looked up and saw a woman standing on the path.

"Who are you, most beautiful?" Az Rex excitedly questioned, hoping it was the woman in the tower.

He hoped she escaped, and they could leave the island at that moment.

"You do not remember me? I am your twin sister, Karisma," she softly answered.

"The insane old man, and now you. I don't have a sister," Az Rex said with a dumb-looking smirk on his face. "You must know, there are punishments for lying to a king."

Karisma pleaded back, "Remember back to when we were children, our trips to the caves on the beach. The times we spent riding horses together."

Az Rex thought hard but remembered nothing. Then after a few minutes, he thought of the drawings on the cave wall.

"Can this be true? Why would no one have any remembrance of you?"

"I was taken here, to this beautiful island, as a punishment to our parents because of the wars," answered Karisma.

Az Rex questioned, "What wars? There have never been any wars in the kingdom."

"The wars which were fought over me. Princes and knights fought over who would marry me. Our father refused to stop the wars. Ulric, the wizard, created this island for me to watch over and protect its magic. I can never leave this island," Karisma frantically explained.

Az Rex, with his eyes turning red and a giant-sized smirk, exclaimed, "This is impossible. I will slay the beast, and you will be my slave as a punishment for your lies. There have been no wars. I have no sister, and I can use a slave with your beauty."

"You are lost, you need help. Please listen. I can save you from your rage," begged Karisma with tears starting to fall down her cheeks.

"Bow before your new master," Az Rex commanded as he reached for his sword. "If you do not bow down, my sword will teach you a lesson in obedience."

Karisma looked at Az Rex, and in an instant, she vanished back to her tower. She moved to look out the window and started to cry, "Please listen to me, Az Rex. I love you."

As Karisma cried, clouds built up, and the rain fell. The rain slowed Az Rex's hike through the pass. When he made it to the east shore of the lake, he decided to set up camp and wait out the rain. He used the same campsite as Oton the Fierce and his men. The day turned into night, and the rain showed no signs of stopping. Az Rex spent the night sharpening his sword and resting, waiting for the rain to stop. All he could think about was obtaining his magical slave. With her in his kingdom, nothing would stop him from becoming powerful. The night turned into day, and the rain kept falling.

Karisma, sitting in her room, decided that it was time to put an end to Az Rex and his rage.

"My parents' kingdom is gone. My twin brother will never remember me," she said, looking in the mirror. "This terror ends today."

Karisma jumped out of the window and changed into the lake monster. She quickly made her way east, toward the campsite.

The rain stopped, Az Rex, growing short on patience, started to head west. He desperately wanted his slave girl, and he wanted the lake monster dead. The monster's head would make a great trophy on any wall, but in his palace above his throne would show his great power to any kingdom. The rage burned in his eyes, and his body shook with anger as he walked toward the tower.

Az Rex glanced at the lake and saw the monster swimming toward him. He raised his bow and shot an arrow at the lake monster. The arrow missed. Karisma shot a fireball toward Az Rex. Az Rex jumped to the side, and the fireball flew by him, just missing his right arm. He continued to make his way toward the tower, shooting arrows each time he saw the monster pop up in the lake.

As he approached the tower, a large fireball landed in front of him. The fire from the fireball surrounded him. Karisma appeared in front of him.

"Az Rex, this is your last chance. Leave this island, remove the lust for power in your life, and you will live. If not, you will die," she demanded.

"My slave, you are delusional. That will never happen. You used magic. *Now* you will become my slave, or you will die," Az Rex responded and tightly grabbed his sword.

Karisma reached toward Az Rex's sword and, with the help of her magic, knocked it out of his grasp. She grabbed it off the ground and raised it up. Az Rex jumped toward her, with his hands in a fist. The sword stuck in Az Rex's chest.

With a look of surprise on his face, he said, "Karisma?"

"Yes, Az Rex?" softly responded Karisma while she held her brother in her arms.

The flames around the two vanished.

"I remember now." Az Rex coughed. "I am sorry. I beg you, please forgive me."

Karisma looked into his face and said, "I love you, Az Rex."

Az Rex looked at her, smiled, and took his last breath. Karisma held her brother for what seemed like days. She wept, but this time the sun shone brightly. Her brother was redeemed!

CHAPTER 12

Karisma's Island

Karisma buried her brother at the campsite on the east shore of the lake. She used her magic to grow a special flower, one that would grow and bloom through all seasons. It had midnight-blue petals with a bright-yellow center. The flower was about six inches across, from petal to petal. The stem and leaves were a dark forest green, and it was about eight inches tall. Karisma also made some trees that would encircle the grave. She wanted no one to find or disturb the final resting place of Az Rex. She placed his sword in his hands as a final symbol of his royalty.

Karisma made her way back to her tower. She thought of her brother often, but she started to think about her three other brothers. She only saw them once, right after they were born. When she left, they were one. At the time of Az Rex's death, they were three. Ulric promised they were safe. She wanted to make sure that they didn't become filled with evil as did Az Rex had. She used her magic to check up on them. She saw the three of them running around a small sand house. The people looked poor, but to Karisma, this was good and for their best interest. It was completely different than what Az Rex had grown up with.

Three years later, Karisma appeared to her brothers in a dream. Her image shone like a bright star. She pointed to the north, toward a castle ruin. She hoped that someday they would make it there, to the place where they were born. She left a gift there for them. The gift would teach them about their short past in royalty. She also gave each brother a special gift that each would be able to use as they grew up. One was given the gift of farming the land. He would be able to grow and use any kind of plant. One was given the gift of handling wealth. He would be able to use money in a responsible way, a way that would not turn into greed. The third was given the gift of peace. He would be able to control people in such a way that peace would remain. Karisma disappeared from the dream. She hoped that they would be able to use what she had given them in their future.

Karisma stayed in the tower for fifteen years. She kept learning and teaching herself how to use her magic for good. She hoped that someday her brothers would travel to the island. She wondered and thought about the prophecy. *Who is the one that will unite the island? What does that mean? How will the island become separated?* These were questions that Karisma pondered and meditated on each and every day. One thing she knew, everything Ulric taught her had come true. She knew she would be needed once again; she just had to wait until that day.

In the years following the death of Az Rex, the legend of the island faded from everyone's memory, just like Ulric, the great wizard of the wolf tribe, had told her. Princess Karisma, the lake monster, and the island were all forgotten.

PART II

Fifteen years passed by since the time of the death of Az Rex. Karisma had matched Ulric in magical knowledge and strength. She found that his books and scrolls were not in his hut when Az Rex burned it, so she passed the time by reading and learning. Not much more is known about what happened at this time, other than Karisma kept watch on her brothers. The brothers grew, but being in an extremely poor family, no one cared to document what went on in their lives. No one would have come to guess that they were royalty from another kingdom. By the time they were eighteen, she knew it was time for them to come to her island.

CHAPTER 13

The Brothers

"Did you find any money?" asked a boy, with short, curly black hair and deep dark-brown eyes.

He was shorter and stalker than most boys his age, but he tried to keep a nice appearance. His face was always clean-shaven and well groomed. His voice was quiet and sounded like he was from the deep south of America. His clothes used to be white and were well beaten and worn with their age.

"No, not this time, Cass," replied another boy while looking in a purse that he "happened" to find laying in the market.

He had straight, medium-length blond hair that just touched his shoulders and sky-blue eyes. His face was a little scruffy, but being eighteen, that seemed to be the norm. His voice was louder and seemed not to have the accent of Cass. His clothes were a light brown, and just like the other boy's, they were worn out.

"Goran, we need money to buy food, or we will starve to death. I wonder if Salem got something good *playing* cards?" said Cass. "Let's go find our brother and find out if he was able to swindle any money today."

He rubbed his stomach in a way to say that he was hungry.

The two brothers left the alley in the marketplace and made their way to the local saloon to find their brother. The brothers, triplets by birth, were poor and in need of any help they could find. Their parents died when they were extremely young, and their caretakers were among the poorest in the land. It was by some sort of divine intervention that they had enough to eat each night. For seventeen years, the brothers longed to find out about their parents, but they were always given no answers when they asked about their parents.

The two made their way to the entrance of the saloon and peeped inside the door. They saw Salem. He was tall and muscular. He had long brown hair and almost-black eyes. He had a small beard that was neatly trimmed at all times. He wore black loose-fitting clothes that were in better shape than his brothers. He spoke like he was more educated than his brothers. He had no accents, and his voice was just average, not overbearing.

Each brother had their own special ability. Goran was able to keep track of money, which right now was almost nothing. He could look at a person and know exactly how much money they were carrying. He was able to win a lot by being able to guess what people had in their pockets. Over time, people stopped playing because they thought he was cheating them. Cass knew the land. He was able to grow any crop in any type of soil. His only problem was that they had no money to afford to buy any seeds. And when he could get some seeds, there wasn't enough water in the desert city to keep anything alive. Salem was the only one that could keep the three of them together. He knew what to say and was able to keep the peace between them.

As Cass and Goran looked inside, they saw two guards dragging Salem to the back of the saloon.

"Again?" Cass asked while looking at Goran.

The two walked calmly through the door and made their way to where the guards were heading. They did not want to cause a giant scene of commotion. The guards were wearing helmets and some lighter armor. One had keys hanging on the front of his armor and wore an important-looking green sash over his armor.

"This is the last time that you steal from the people here," the more-important-looking guard commanded to Salem.

The guard pulled his arm up and made Salem stand face-to-face with him.

"I didn't steal anything. I won the money fair in a poker game," pleaded Salem.

The guard slapped Salem.

"Don't lie to me boy," he yelled as he lifted Salem's shirt up.

Some playing cards fell out of Salem's sleeve and landed with five aces of hearts laying face up. The guard smiled and seized the opportunity to tie Salem's hands behind his back.

The main guard who was holding Salem looked at the other guard and said, "Take him to the town center. Cut his hand off, the penalty for stealing from these good people. Make sure there is a large crowd of people so they can see this example of dishonesty and thievery."

"Yes, sir," the young guard said with some arrogance in his voice.

He shoved Salem toward the door and forced him out of the saloon onto the main city street.

Cass and Goran snuck out the back door and ran onto the street.

Cass said quietly to Goran, "We need to save our brother."

The two ran ahead of the guard, and Cass stopped in the middle of the road. He fell over and clutched his head in his hands.

Goren, trying not to laugh, yelled, "Help, my brother is sick! He needs help!"

The guard forced Salem to the ground and commanded him to stay on the ground and ran over to give Cass some aid. When he arrived and looked down, Cass stood up and punched him in the head. The guard fell, knocked out cold. Goran ran behind Salem and untied his hands.

"Thank you, my brothers," said Salem. "I knew you two would not let me down. I do have some money in my shoe. It is not a lot, but it will buy some food for tonight."

Cass interrupted, "I think we need to leave here. The guards will be looking for all of us now."

"Good idea, Cass," said Salem. "Let's go home and get our belongings. It won't take long to grab all we have. Then we can travel north. Hopefully, we can find something better there."

The three brothers ran home as fast as they could. When they arrived a few minutes later, "Hello, boys," was heard from their mother, the lady in charge of taking care of them when they were babies.

"Hello, Mama," Salem calmly said.

"What did you boys do this time?" Mama asked.

Their mama was a short and skinny lady, who worked extremely hard for everything they had. It wasn't much, but they always had a roof over their heads and an extremely small amount food on the table. Her hair was long and dark with grey streaks. Her skin was almost a leathery color, and her eyes were light blue.

"Nothing, Mama," said Cass, hiding something in his eyes.

Mama, with a look of disbelief, said, "When are you boys going to learn? You are only hurting yourselves. Your real parents would be very disappointed with how you are turning out. You need to be men of high honor and integrity."

"How do you know that? Who are our parents? You never tell us anything about our parents," screamed Goran with some bitter anger in his voice.

"I know," Mama sadly said, "but I am not allowed to say anything for your safety."

"You always say that. We are old enough to take care of ourselves now. Please, tell us," demanded Salem.

"I cannot," Mama said. "I wish I could."

"Fine," yelled Goran as the three walked out of the small two-room hut.

"Where are you going to go?" Mama tearfully asked.

Salem rashly replied, "Away from here. Thank you for taking care of us. Goodbye."

Mama, knowing that she could not stop them from leaving, cried as they walked away. She quietly prayed that they would be safe and find their answers. She loved them as she would love her own children if she had any, and she knew deep down that they loved her.

CHAPTER 14

The Path North

"Do you think we will ever learn where we came from and why our parents are kept a secret from us?" asked Cass as the boys left the city. "Maybe they were great rulers from a great kingdom?"

Goran, the strongest of the three, punched Cass in the arm at the last comment and said, "You know that is not true. No one could keep that a secret."

"Someday, maybe we will find where we came from," replied Salem in a sad but hopeful tone.

The boys made their way north. The well-traveled path led through fields and forests. Cass had never seen so much green in a field before. The farther north they traveled, the less the path seemed to be traveled and the thicker the forest became. The denseness of the forest caused the travel to slow to almost a crawl.

The sky started to darken into night, and the three boys made a camp in a small clearing. Salem made a fire, Cass found some walnuts, and Goran made a makeshift tent for them to sleep in. They ate and told some jokes to each other, and some punches were thrown after a few of the jokes. After a couple of hours of this, the boys drifted off to sleep.

That night, a storm blew in from the north. The rain found some places to leak in the tent, but the boys stayed dry for the most part. The constant and never-ending flashes of lightning scared the three. Cass swore he heard their names being called in the thunder. He asked a few times, "Did you hear that?" Salem and Goran picked on him for hearing things until the lightning struck a few yards away.

The thunder was deafening, but the words, "Goran, Cass, Salem," were heard clearly. The boys were stunned and scared, but found the courage and crawled out of the tent. Before them stood a beautiful lady with long, dark hair and midnight-blue eyes. She looked to be about twenty years old. There was a glowing blue aroura that surrounded her.

"Hello, Goran, Cass, and Salem. Why did you not come when I first called you? I called to you many times tonight," said the mysterious lady.

"Salem and I did not hear you, and we made fun of Cass for hearing our names. What do you want with us? Why are you calling us? Please don't hurt us. We will behave from now on," Goran pleaded and begged.

The lady smiled and replied, "I am not here to harm you. You will continue your travel to the north, to ruins of what used to be a great and glorious castle. There you will be able to learn about who you are and where you come from."

Cass interrupted the lady as she spoke, "How do you know who we are?"

The lady slowly vanished and softly said, "Remember my instructions."

As she vanished, the storm immediately stopped, and the stars shone brightly.

"Umm, I guess we will keep heading north," said Salem.

The other two boys, with mouths wide opened, nodded their head in complete agreement.

The three left their campsite after a couple of hours of restless sleep. The sun was just peaking over the horizon, and the moon was starting to set. It was a beautiful sight, one that Cass took the time to look at in amazement.

"Are you coming?" loudly questioned Goran.

Cass answered Goran back with a roll of his eyes and a dumb-looking smile. He ran the few yards and caught up with his brothers.

The walk was painfully long and hard. The path, or what used to be a path, was overgrown with large trees and thick bushes. The branches seemed to intertwine with other branches. Salem wished he had a sword so he could cut the branches.

"How much farther is this castle? My legs are tired," complained Cass.

"I don't know. If you ask again, I will punch you in the nose," answered Goran.

Salem interrupted, "Why can't you two get along? We have no rules now. It is just us."

"Shut your mouth, Salem," argued Goran. He turned toward Salem and…

Whack.

A branch, swung by Cass, hit Goran in the back of the head. Goran fell down to his knees, holding his head in his hands.

"What was that for?"

"You need to shut *your* mouth," sternly answered Cass.

Salem, looking at his brothers and laughing, said, "Are you two ready to continue the journey? We don't need to waste any more energy on foolish things."

Goran stood to his feet and started to walk on the path, keeping his mouth shut. Cass dropped his stick and walked next to Goran. Salem, pleased that his brothers wised up, followed close behind.

The brutal day finally came to an end, and the three set up their camp once more. After a nice meal of freshly caught rabbit, Goran and Salem fell asleep quickly. Cass, looking into the stars, was in a deep thought. "Cass, come here," was heard in the distance. Cass stood up, looked around, and then walked toward the voice.

"Yes. I am here," quietly replied Cass.

The same lady from the night before stood before Cass.

"Your journey is near an end. Tomorrow you will find the castle. Look for clues. They will tell you who you are."

"What clues?" eagerly questioned Cass. "What are you talking about?"

"You will know when you find them," the mysterious lady said.

"Please, tell me. I don't want to wait another day to find the answers to what we have been wanting our whole lives," said Cass.

He waited for a response, but the lady was gone with a quick flash.

Cass went back to the campsite, stoked the fire, and drifted off to a restless sleep. When he finally got to sleep for the night, he dreamed of a giant castle, with a king, queen, princess, prince, and three young babies. He dreamed of a war that took the princess away. He dreamed of a second war that destroyed the castle and the family that lived in it. Cass awoke the next morning to a bucket of water being poured on his head. He quickly jumped up at the shock and saw Goran holding the bucket.

"Don't you ever hit me with a stick again," Goran said with wide-open eyes and a shady-looking smile.

During a quick breakfast of blueberries, Cass told the others about that lady appearing to him during the night. He told them about his dream. None of them had an answer to what the dream meant. After pondering the dream for a few minutes, the boys continued on their journey.

CHAPTER 15

What the Boys Found

A few hours later, about high noon, the boys found a badly burned wall that was covered in trees and vines. A few stones had fallen off of the wall, but it was mostly intact. The boys looked at it and made their way to the other side of the wall. Here they found what could be the rest of a castle. It was in total ruins, just stones piles upon stones. Nothing was left standing. What appeared to be an old-looking throne was sticking out in the middle of the rubble.

Cass walked toward the throne, near the center of the ruins, which he believed would be the throne room. The rubble shifted and swallowed Cass down into a dark shaft.

"Cass!" screamed Salem.

Salem ran toward the spot his brother fell but could not find the shaft. It seemed to magically disappear. Goran ran to where Salem was and aided in the search of where Cass was swallowed up.

Cass landed on his back with a loud thud. After a moment, he regained his breath and thoughts. He stood up and looked around. A small stream of light poked into the room. The light pointed toward a torch that was hanging on the wall. Cass, thinking that he was in luck, grabbed the torch and managed to light a fire with the small piece of flint he has in his pocket. The torch showed some light, but it was still dark. Cass looked around again, and he could see that he was in a hallway. Behind him were some stairs up, but they were blocked by the debris from the castle. In front of him, the hallway seemed to go on for miles.

Cass made his way slowly down the hallway. There were many large wooden doors on each side of the hallway, but each one was blocked and unable to open. At the end of the hallway was a large wooden door. Cass pushed all weight on the door, trying to make it budge. Unfortunately for Cass, the door flung open with ease. When the door flew open, Cass fell through it landing on his face. His torch flew out of his hand and landed somewhere in the room. When it landed, the torch extinguished itself, leaving a dark room for Cass. Cass laid on the floor for a minute, regaining his breath once again and this time trying not to laugh at what just happened.

Cass stood up and tried to look around the dark room, trying to see if he could make out anything. He felt his way around the wall and found a couple more torches that he lit. As the room lit up, Cass was amazed at what he found. The room was round in shape and seemed to be a giant treasure room, filled with gold, armor, weapons, books, and scrolls. In the middle of the scrolls was a map of an island. On the back of the map, the names Ulric, Oton the Fierce, and Az Rex were written. The map showed the location of a tower on the island. Cass folded the map and put it in his pocket. Something inside of him told him that it was very important.

Cass looked at the far side and saw a large paper hanging. The paper looked like a family tree. Cass walked to look at it; he noticed that his name, along with his brothers, was listed on it. According to the paper, the three had an older brother and sister who were twins, Az Rex and Karisma. All five of them were of royalty, one princess and four princes. *Could this be true? Could I be right?* he thought. Cass grabbed the paper off the wall. He wanted to show his brothers what he found, that is, if he could ever find a way out.

Cass turned around and saw the mysterious lady from the previous two nights, standing in the doorway.

"Did you find what you were looking for?" she asked.

"What was I looking for?" Cass questioned back.

The lady answered, "You have a map of an island in your pocket and a family tree in your hand."

"What can you tell me about these papers?" asked Cass.

"Ask me what you want to know, and I will tell you what I can," the mysterious lady answered.

Cass thought for a quick moment and then asked, "First off, who are you?"

The lady spoke softly, "I am Karisma, your sister. I have been watching over you for many years. I led you, Cass, to this room so you could find the answers you have searched for those many years."

"My sister?" Cass excitedly asked. "But you are barely older than I am. How can this be?"

"It is through magic that I do not age. I am using magic to appear to you," Karisma answered.

Cass continued his questions, "Why would you appear to me? My brother, Salem, is wiser than I am, and Goran is stronger."

"You are the one that is most humble. You see things in a different way. Your eyes are open to wonderful things. Your brothers only see what is in front of them. Remember the sunrise two mornings ago? How you stood still and admired the beauty of it? Your brothers wanted to move on quickly to start the day's journey." Karisma waved her hand, and the sunset was recreated in the room.

"How are you my sister when I have no memory of having a sister?" Cass asked in a serious tone. "Is this some sort of a trick?"

Karisma answered, and some soft tears welled up in her eyes, "I was taken away when you were one, just babies. There was a war happening, a war that our father would not stop. I was taken away as a punishment for the war."

"What about Az Rex? Who is that?" Cass asked, trying to take in all that he had learned so far.

Karisma sadly answered, "He was my twin and our brother. He was destined to be king to this very castle, but he was overcome with the lust for power. He was killed for the damage he caused to many innocent people."

"What happened to the castle? Where are the king and queen?" Cass questioned with more curiosity but also fearing he knew the answer in his heart.

With tears falling down her cheeks, Karisma answered, "As a final punishment to the king and queen, our father and mother, the kingdom was taken away from them. The king was killed by Az Rex in a fit of rage. The queen was killed when the kingdom was destroyed."

Cass, feeling a bit depressed, continued his questions, "How did we, my brothers and I, survive?"

Karisma, sadly looking toward the ground, answered, "You were taken, before the final battle, to a faraway city to be hidden. That is why you could not learn who you were, until now, when the time was right. Follow the map in your pocket. Come to my island. There you three will fulfill the promise made to our father, which was that his heir will forever sit on a throne. I must go know. Remember, follow the map. It will guide you there."

Karisma vanished, and the stones that blocked the stairway disappeared. Cass ran out of the room, down the hallway, and up the stairs to find his brothers still searching for the place that he fell.

"Salem! Goran! I have great news for you!" yelled Cass. "We are princes. This used to be our parent's castle."

"Ya, right," Goran said with a sarcastic voice. "You must have hit your head pretty hard on that fall. What did I tell you last time?"

Cass, defending himself, said, "No, the lady in the vision is our sister. Her name is Karisma. I have proof that she is our sister. Here is an old family tree that I found hanging on the wall."

Cass reached into his pocket and showed them the paper. Cass told his brothers about the whole encounter with Karisma. He explained the wars and why they were taken away.

"Why not go? We have nothing here to lose," replied Salem after Cass showed the map to them. "I don't know about you, but there is nothing left here for me to see."

Salem heard stories of a great harbor city to the east. The boys talked it over and eventually started their way to the harbor to sail to the island. They needed to either buy a boat, with no money to their name, or convince a sailor to take them to the island. The problem with having a sailor take them was that they would have to explain the whole story to them. Goran didn't want to share the island with anyone. Cass was excited to finally meet his sister face-to-face. Salam thought they should be cautious with what they did.

CHAPTER 16

To the Island

After a long couple of days walking, the exhausted boys made it to the harbor. They found lots of ships that would sail them to an island, but the cost was out of their price range. Buying a boat was also too costly. They were offered jobs for pay, but they didn't have much patience and wanted to continue the journey quickly.

Goran left the other two and walked down the main pier. Cass and Salem continued to talk to sailors, hoping that they could find someone that would take them. An hour later, Goran ran quietly and grabbed his brothers.

"Follow me, I found something you might like," he quietly murmured.

The three quietly made their way to a small pier. There was a small ship tied to the dock. It was already ready to set sail. No one was on, or even near, the dock or in the ship.

"I found our way to the island," Goran said with a giant smile.

"You want us to steal a ship?" a puzzled Cass questioned. "I thought we all agreed that we were going to stop this behavior."

"If there is no one around, then it deserves to be taken," eagerly answered Goran. "Don't you want to go the island? This is easy. I walked around inside the ship. There is nobody inside of it. It is full of supplies and ready to go. It could be a *magical* gift. Our sister has been guiding us all along."

"This might be our best and only chance," replied Salem, not exactly excited about the situation but also seeing it as a good opportunity.

"I don't know. Remember that Karisma sees all that we do. This is not right, and you know it," argued Cass.

"Salem and I are going. Are you going to join us?" questioned Goran, knowing that Cass would eventually give up his protest and join them on the adventure.

Cass followed his brothers on the ship and helped them untie the ropes so they could leave on the journey to the island. When the ropes were untied, the ship started to move slowly. Goran lowered the sails, and Salem steered the ship out of the port. Salem was a natural when it came to sailing. He practiced many times in the small lake by the city where the brothers grew up. The lake would appear once a year after the one month of rain. If he had money, he would have bought a boat. Jokingly, people would call him a land pirate because there was no ocean by the city. Now Salem was behind the wheel of a real ship, on one that they stole, making him a real pirate.

The ship was small compared to a lot of the others at the harbor, but it was easily manageable for the three of them. It had only one mainsail. It had spots for five cannons, but they only found one.

"I hope we don't need to use this cannon. If we do, we will be outnumbered," Cass sarcastically stated the obvious.

Cass took the wheel, and after some quick instructions from Salem, he held a straight course. Salem took the time to explore the captain's quarters. There he found three small chests of gold, a very large bed, a desk with some maps, and many bottles of rum.

Goran explored the lower deck. The main room had nine hammocks against the wall. They were stacked three high. There were three on each side wall and three against the far wall. The far wall also had a door that led to the cargo hold. In the cargo hold, he found some barrels of black powder, some crates that had fine china, some food, and lots of rum. The boys never had drunk rum before. Goran took a case of rum to the upper deck and poured a large glass for each of them.

"Drink up, boys. If we are going to be pirates, then we should drink like them," he exclaimed, eager for his first taste of rum.

The first sip of rum was a surprise to them. Goran shrieked like a boy getting kicked by a mule as the rum went down his throat. Salem had tears in his eyes. Cass, trying to act tough, ran to the side of the ship and spit the rum over the side into the ocean. Goran saw him spit it out and punched him in the shoulder.

"You are such a lass," Goran mocked Cass while trying to sound like a pirate.

The boys spent the next couple of hours drinking rum and punching each other. Goran couldn't walk around the ship. He stumbled and fell. Eventually, he just gave up and fell asleep in the middle of the deck. Salem was not much better. He did make it to the bed in the captain's quarters, but only made it halfway in the bed. His knees were on the floor, and his head was on the bed. Cass just sat next to the mast. He had a bucket next to him that he used a few times when he got sick.

The next day, the boys woke up feeling like they had been in a large battle.

"I am never touching rum again," said Cass, still holding the bucket.

"I completely agree with you," replied Goran, holding his head tightly and hoping it would not explode.

Salem made his way out of the room.

"The sun is too bright," he mumbled and squinted tightly. "My head feels like it was split in half with an ax."

A few hours later, the boys felt fine. The rum was a distant memory. The short-term memory of Goran was apparent and on display when he ran across the deck with a bottle of rum in his hand.

Using the map in the captain's quarters and the map that Cass obtained, Salem charted a course that hopefully would lead them to the island. Salem carefully steered the ship back on course. With only one sail, the trip would take a few days. He hoped that the journey was worth what they went through to get this far.

Cass prepared a meal for all them to enjoy. He made some steaks and potatoes from the supplies that were found. The boys sat down and enjoyed their meal, which might have been one of the finest they had ever had.

Goran asked, "You said that we would all be kings. How is that going to work? You know I am stronger. I would conquer both of you and rule the island for myself."

Salem, with a little anger, replied, "But you are not smart. I would use my brains and find a way to win and rule the island."

"Come on, guys. We are in this together. We are brothers. We can figure out how to rule together," responded Cass. This statement was met with a punch in the arm by Goran. "Ouch!" he screamed as he stared at Goran.

"Told you that I am stronger," Goran smiled and put his feet on the table.

As the three argued into the evening, a storm started to grow. The lightning was a familiar midnight-blue color. The thunder rocked the ship. The waves covered the deck. Goran hid in great fear below deck. Cass and Salem did what they could to keep the ship on course. The waves became higher and crashed with more force. The lightning seemed to never stop. Goran appeared next to the wheel.

"We are going to die!" he screamed.

"I told you that we should not have stolen the ship," reprimanded Cass.

"Both of you stop. We will be fine," Salem hopefully said while interrupting his brothers.

A moment later, a wave crashed through the deck, and the ship broke into many pieces. Goran grabbed both of his brothers and used his legs to swim to a large piece of what was left of the deck.

"This will keep us afloat," said Goran as he climbed on the wood.

Minutes felt like hours; hours felt like days. The storm had no end in sight. Cass laid on his back and looked through the rain and up into the clouds.

"Karisma, please save us," he yelled with great fear. "You wanted us to come. Please help us."

Cass closed his eyes. A large lightning bolt landed next to them with a deafening roar of thunder. A second later, the storm cleared up. The sky was bright and sunny, with no clouds left in the sky.

Salem looked to the east.

"Look over there in the distance. There is an island. We will be safe there," he said.

Goran replied, "I should have saved some rum."

Cass looked at his brother and kicked him off the wood into the water. As Goran splashed into the water, he grabbed Salem's leg and pulled him off as well. Cass looked at his brothers swimming to catch up and smiled ear to ear.

CHAPTER 17

Meeting Karisma

The broken and splintered deck board glided slowly to the shore of the island. When the wreckage got close to the shore, the brothers jumped off and walked through the gentle ocean waves to the sandy shore. Standing one hundred feet inland from them was a lady wearing a medium-length, light-blue dress. She had long, dark hair. She waved to the brothers to come to her.

They came closer to the lady, and Cass in a gentle voice asked, "Karisma?"

The lady smiled and said, "Hello, my brothers. Welcome to your new home."

Cass gave Karisma a hug and introduced her to Salem and Goran. Salem also embraced his sister. Goran stood with his mouth open and staring at her.

"Close your mouth. I am your sister," she playfully said. "Let me show you around the island. There are many things that you will love here. Climb on my back."

Karisma changed into a dragon, to the amazement of the brothers. The only thing that resembled Karisma were her dark, midnight-blue eyes. Cass climbed on first, followed by Salem, then Goran.

Karisma took off and headed to the north. She showed them the thick and luscious forest area. The boys had never seen so many trees in one place. She headed back south, showing the fertile fields. The fields were different colors of greens and golds. Then she turned to the west. There she showed them the gold-filled mountains. The rocky cliffs would scare anyone looking over the tops of them. They spotted a couple waterfalls in the mountains. She explained that each region was vastly different from the others.

"The island is a great source of magic and resources. Use these both wisely. If you do, your kingdoms will last forever. Do you understand, Goran?"

Goran, looking both puzzled and embarrassed, quickly responded, "Yes, I understand, but why do you single me out?"

"You have it in your heart to always be the one in charge of your brothers because of your strength. For the island to prosper, you need your brothers. You all need to work as one," Karisma taught as they flew through the open air.

After a flight over the mountains, she took them to a lake near the mountains.

"This is a sacred place, a magical hot spring. The item that created this whole island lies beneath the water of this hot springs. Do not ever go in search of this item, and do not reveal what is here to anyone. This is your one and only warning," Karisma said with all seriousness in her voice.

The boys shook their head to agree with what Karisma just told them.

After a quick stop at the hot springs, Karisma brought them to her tower by Kingsbridge Lake. Salem looked down and pointed out all the rusted armor by the lake. Karisma landed and changed back into her human form.

"Can we learn to do that?" asked Cass.

"No, you will not learn to use the magic. You were not chosen for magic, but you three will protect the magic, and in turn, you have been chosen to rule the island together," Karisma answered.

Karisma set up a camp for them by the tower. She cooked a big dinner for all of them to enjoy with the fresh trout she caught from Kingsbridge Lake. She also made a fruit salad with the blueberries, strawberries, and blackberries from the bushes in the forest. During dinner, Karisma answered many questions about her growing up. She told them about their parents. She told them the story of Az Rex. The boys had many questions, and Karisma took the time to answer all of them.

Karisma finished by saying, "Tomorrow each one of you will face a trial. If you pass, you will become a king on this island."

"What if we fail?" questioned Goran.

Karisma replied and sincerely said, "Goran, you always think of the worst possibility, but if you do fail, you will be vanished away from this island. Forever, never to return."

Salem asked, "Do we get any training to prepare us?"

"No. Everything you need is already inside of you. You will know what to do when the times come," answered Karisma with excitement in her eyes. "Get some rest tonight. The trials will start tomorrow. Drink this tea. It will help you relax and get a good night's rest."

Karisma handed each one of the boys a cup of tea. They all drank the tea and turned in for the night. The stars shone brightly overhead. Cass never knew there could be so many stars. The moon was a perfect crescent of silver that hung on the horizon.

"What do you think?" asked Cass.

"The island is beautiful. I look forward to showing that I can be a king," replied Salem.

"Our sister is extremely pretty," added Goran.

"Is that all you have to say?" Cass said while rolling his eyes.

The three drifted off to sleep. There was not much movement until early morning when they were greeted with a gentle-sounding, "Good morning," from Karisma. She had breakfast of fresh eggs and warm bread waiting for them.

The brothers ate the extremely good food and then got ready for the day. They each would go to a separate region of the island and face separate trials. Karisma could not help them and would not allow them to be in touch with each other. They were all on their own, something that they had never done before.

After everyone was ready, the four met in front of the tower. Karisma gave them simple directions. She waved her hand, and the brothers vanished into thin air.

CHAPTER 18

Cass's Trial

Cass appeared on the southern shore. He took his shoes off so he could feel the warm sand. It felt good on his feet as he walked along the shore. The salty smell of the ocean air made him smile. He looked around and thought of what was to come. Cass walked around the beach and thought of all the beauty that surrounded him, the sand, the ocean, the fields to the east, and the three quarters of the risen sun appearing out of the ocean.

Karisma appeared on the shore and walked toward Cass.

"What do you think of this area?" she asked.

"It is beautiful. This might be the perfect place to watch the sunrise," Cass responded with the look of someone who has found peace.

"Someday you will have a palace in this spot. All you have to do is pass the trial. Don't give into temptation. Use your wisdom," Karisma warned and instructed.

"What is my tr..."—as the word came out of Cass's mouth, Karisma disappeared—"...ial?"

Cass, now alone, walked around the beach. He made his way to the fields. He was startled as some blackbirds shot up out of the grass.

"Cass, come here," he heard behind a large tree that was standing alone near the start of the fields. Cass looked carefully and saw nothing. The voice repeated, "Cass, come here."

Cass cautiously walked to the tree.

"Who are you?" he asked with some fear in his voice.

"Cass, over here," came from the tall grass in the field.

Cass kept following the voice. Each time he got to where the voice was, the voice came from another place.

The voice led Cass to the river. A tall knight was sitting on the river bank.

The knight looked Cass in the eyes and said in a deep voice, "Cass, I need your help. Come here, and I will tell you what I need."

The knight was in his full silver armor. His helmet sparkled in the sunlight, and his gloves looked well used. His silver boots were mud-stained on the toes.

"What do you need help with?" asked Cass with the curiosity of a ten-year-old on his first quest.

"I need to find a hot spring. I have heard a legend that there is magical water there, and I need the water to heal myself. I was injured in a vicious battle, and the water can heal me."

"Magical water? In a hot spring? On this island?" Cass questioned with a smug tone.

"Yes, the water is known to heal the sick. Where is this magical water? Please tell me, I beg you to tell. Look at my hands. The injury has caused them to keep shaking," the knight pleaded.

Cass responded to the knight's plea for help, "I cannot tell you about this hot spring, but I do know how to heal your injury. There is a plant called Yarrow. This plant can be made into a tea. The tea will help you to get feeling better."

"Can you show me this plant?" the puzzled knight asked.

"Yes, come with me. There is plenty of Yarrow in the fields."

Cass got up and waved his hand for the knight to follow. The knight slowly rose from his seat on the river bank and limped toward Cass. Cass and the knight walked a few yards into the field. Cass stopped and picked some small white flowers.

"Make some tea out of these flowers and drink the tea. This will heal you," Cass instructed as he handed the flowers to the knight.

"Thank you, Cass, and good luck with the rest of your trial. You acted wisely by finding a solution to the problem without giving up the magic of the hot springs," the knight happily said as he walked out of the field and disappeared into the sandy, tall grass.

"Was that my trial?" Cass wondered.

Cass walked back to the river and washed his face. The cool water felt good after walking through the sun-filled field. Cass sat down for a minute to think about what he just went through.

"Cass, I need your help," was heard coming from down the river path. The voice sounded very familiar to him. He quickly walked east along the river path and found his brother, Goran, sitting on a large rock. "It's about time you got here. I need your help with my trial."

"What do you need help with, Goran? I am in the middle of mine," asked an extremely confused Cass.

"I need to find a flower. As you know, I cannot swim too well. I know you can swim, so could you please help me get this flower?" Goran demanded.

"Sure, I guess I can help you finish your trial. Brothers need to help each other. Where do we need to go?" Cass happily replied.

Goran answered back and waved his hand, "Follow me, and I will show you."

The two brothers walked west along the river path. After a couple miles the river turned to the north, toward the mountains. The brothers left the river and continued west.

"Hey, you two," was heard directly ahead of them. Cass looked ahead and saw Salem. "What are you two doing here? Why are you not working on your trials?"

Goran proudly answered, "Cass is helping me find a flower that I need to complete my trial."

"Is the flower in the water?" Goran shook his head yes. "I need a petal from the flower for my trial. Cass, can you help me get the flower also? Then we can go and be kings together," asked Salem

"Yes, I can help you both. I think that I have already finished my trial," proudly answered Cass with a large smile.

The three of them continued the journey west. A half mile later, through a dark, dense, and untraveled forest, the boys made it to the water with the flower.

Cass looked at the water and realized that they were at the hot springs.

"We shouldn't be here," he fearfully said. "Karisma instructed us to avoid this hot springs and flower inside."

"Don't you want to help us finish our trials, or do you want to be king by yourself?" Goran said with an evil glare in his eyes.

"Come on, I need that flower petal to pass my trial. Karisma told me to get it for her," begged Salem.

Cass responded, "Why would she tell you that? Karisma told us not to be here. You clearly heard her."

"My trial is to get the flower. I don't know why, but she gave it to me," angrily said Goran. "Please help me. I really need the flower."

"*No!*" screamed Cass.

"But you always help your brothers. Get the flower, *now*," demanded Salem.

"No, not this time. Karisma gave us specific instructions, to *never* do this. I will not help get the flower. If you want it, get it yourself," a red-faced Cass yelled.

As soon as he finished yelling, his brothers vanished into a blue mist, and Karisma appeared, standing next to Cass.

Karisma looked proudly at Cass and said, "You stood up to your brothers. You did not give in to them. Good job. This is a lesson that you needed to learn. Do not always give in to them, stand up for your beliefs." She smiled at Cass and happily said, "You have passed your trial."

"Thank you, Karisma," answered Cass, shaking from the encounter with his brothers.

"I will now take you back to the tower," Karisma said.

The two of them vanished and appeared next to the tower door. Cass, regaining his composure, looked around the area and saw his brothers walking toward him.

CHAPTER 19

Goran's Trial

Goran appeared in a lightly grown forest somewhere in the mountains. He took a few brief moments to look around and enjoy the rocky cliffs around him. The cliffs dropped and more mountains rose out of the valley. There was a clearing on the mountain which surrounded by some trees. The trees were white pines that looked thin due to the rocky soil.

Goran started to slowly walk toward a clearing just outside of the forest, and suddenly tripped over something. Goran landed on his face with a giant thud. Embarrassed, he looked around and remembered that he was alone. He examined what he tripped over and found a large stone sticking out of the ground. He examined the stone and found it to be a chunk of gold. Goran, excited to find gold, dug around the lump. The more he dug, the farther down the gold went. The more the gold went down, the more curious he was to know how far it went down.

"Somebody, anyone, please help me! Can anyone hear me?" came from a voice that was heard from inside the trees next to the clearing.

Goran reluctantly got up from his digging and ran toward the voice.

"Who is there? What do you need?" Goran yelled, hoping to hear an answer.

"I am over here," said the voice from the trees.

Goran ran to the trees and saw a young boy standing alone.

"What do you need? How can I help you?" Goran asked while trying to catch his breath from the run.

"I am lost, and I have not eaten anything in days."

The boy was wearing green pants and a stained white shirt. Both parts of his clothing had small tears, not nothing out of the ordinary for a young boy that looked like he was eight or nine. His eyes were light blue, and his face was dirty. His hair was dark and scruffy-looking, like he had never brushed it.

"Where are your parents?" slowly questioned Goran after he got his breath back.

The boy answered with tear welling in his eyes, "I was hunting with my father. I followed a large deer, and I lost my way back to our camp. I was hoping my father would have come looking for me, but it has been three days. We are very poor, and we have to hunt for food. I fear that he might have left me on my own so he wouldn't have to feed me anymore."

"Don't worry, boy. I will help you. First, let's find that deer and get you some food," Goran proudly answered.

Goran felt a connection to the boy, a strong connection that he could not figure out. Goran and the boy quietly walked through the clearing. At the far end, they spotted a herd of elk.

"Here. Use my bow. I am too weak to shoot," said the boy.

Goran took the bow from the boy and shot an arrow toward the unsuspecting herd. The arrow struck a young elk in the heart, and it fell to the ground.

Goran gathered some wood and started a fire. He used some branches to hold the elk above the fire.

"While the meat cooks, we will go in search of your father," he said to the boy.

The two left and looked around. After a couple of hours, Goran spotted a man in the distance.

"Father!" the boy screamed and ran as fast as he could.

The man turned around and, with a slight look of disappointment, said, "Son, I found you."

Goran caught up to the boy and his father.

"Sir," said Goran, "I have a nice meal cooking by the clearing. I would be honored if you and your son would join me."

The boy's father was old and looked like he was sickened, once being a strong man, now weak and skinny. His clothes were tattered and torn, both his pants and shirt were a faded white cloth. When Goran looked at the man, Goran was surprised that the man looked just like him, just older.

The man agreed, and the three walked to the still cooking elk. Goran and the man talked on the way. Goran found out that the man could not afford to take care of his family. He explained how he was sad that his son wandered off but also kind of hoping that the son would not come back so he would not have to take care of him anymore since it was a struggle to find food for his family.

After a perfect meal of elk, Goran took the man to the gold that he had been digging out.

"Take what you need from this gold. There is more than enough to take care of your family and more. Help yourself to what you want, it is all yours."

"Thank you!" exclaimed the man. "I have no words to describe your kindness."

The man reached for the gold, and he and his son vanished into thin air. Goran looked around, trying to figure out what just happened, and then he remembered the trials. *I didn't think about the trials. I just wanted to take care of the boy. He reminded me of me,* he thought to himself.

Goran walked toward the clearing, and he vanished and appeared next to the sacred hot springs. An old man was sitting on a rock, looking at the water.

Goran walked toward the man, and the man said, "You helped me once, long ago, can you help me once again?"

"I helped you before?" Goran asked, scratching his head in confusion.

"You helped me find my father many years ago when I was lost in the clearing. Now my granddaughter is very sick." Goran looked next to the man a saw a girl lying on a blanket. The girl looked to be around five years old. She had long golden hair and sky-blue eyes. She looked very pale from being sick. The man said with all sincerity, "A flower lies beneath the water. A petal from this flower is the only way to save my granddaughter. I can pay you for this, and I can also repay the gold that you gave my father those many years ago. He used the gold to become a great hunter. People would pay him lots of money to hunt for them. I took over his job when he became too old to hunt. Now we have all the money we need to survive for many generations."

The man looked at his granddaughter and said softly, "I know the prophecy, and you are destined to save the island. This man can help save you so you can fulfill your destiny. The island will need someone to save it."

"I don't know," Goran said with concern building in his heart.

"Please, I know you have a good heart and do not like to see people hurting. Here is a large bag of gold," the man begged.

Goran's jaw dropped, and his eyes lit up as he saw the number of gold coins in the bag. There were more than ten thousand-gold coins.

"But I can't. Karisma told me not to use the flower for anything," Goran pleaded. "We are not allowed, for any reason, to use the water or the flower."

The man replied, "I can give you more gold. Do you want four more bags, just like the first?"

Goran looked at the water. He turned back and looked at the bags of money that were next to his feet. He looked at the man and then looked again at the water. His heart raced, and for the second time in his life, Goran felt scared inside. He did not know what to do or how to act with his fear. He looked at the man once again and felt close to him.

Goran took a deep breath and waded out into the water. He was not a very good swimmer, but eventually, he made his way to the middle of the lake. He took another deep breath and dove into the water. Below him, about ten feet down, was a cave. Not thinking about how long he could hold breath and explore the cave, Goran swam down to the cave entrance. It took a couple of minutes, but

Goran swam into the cave entrance. As he entered, the water vanished, and a dry cave surrounded him. It was like a magical door that held the water back. He thought about that for a moment, but a glowing red object caught his attention.

He slowly walked toward the object, which turned out to be an interesting-looking flower. To Goran, a flower was a flower, but this flower was the most beautiful flower that he had ever seen. It had midnight-blue petals, a light-green stem, and the center glowed red, giving off the glow that lit the whole cave.

Goran pulled a petal off the flower and walked back to the cave entrance. He found the spot where the water met the cave and held his breath and jumped through the magical door. He looked up and found himself next to Salem, on the beach facing the tower.

CHAPTER 20

Salem's Trial

Salem appeared in the forest in the northern part of the island. He walked around and took in all the locations of natural resources that could be used in the future. He found a large iron-ore deposit along the coast. The woods were made of ash, cedar, and oak—all great woods to use to make strong structures. Salem's mind was going in lots of directions on things that he could do with all the resources he kept finding. One of his thoughts was to make a strong navy so he could be able to sail the oceans and protect the island.

Karisma appeared next to Salem, and she spoke softly, "There are lots of resources for you to use. Use them wisely. Use them to help people. Don't give into greed, have a giving spirit. Remember, your name means peace."

"I understand, Karisma," Salem humbly responded.

"If you do, and you pass the trials, you will build a palace here on the shore. You will be able to have your navy. Use it for protection, not for your personal glory." Karisma slowly disappeared as she instructed Salem.

A few minutes later, Salem heard voices coming from the forest. He walked toward the voices and found a family of four sitting in a small clearing.

"Excuse me, kind sir," the man said, "could you help us?"

The man was very poorly dressed, wearing well-worn and torn pants and a shirt that used to be white but was stained with dirt and some other stuff that Salem could not identify. His shoes were non-existent, just straps that protected the ball of his feet. His skin was very pale, and his face looked overworked.

"What do you need help with?" Salem asked. He scratched his head because he was puzzled by where the people came from.

"I need to build a house for my family, and I am very short on wood that is ready to use. Do you have any that I can have? I am poor, and I don't have anything to offer. My wife is pregnant and due at any time. My oldest son was paralyzed from a fall, and my youngest son has been sick for a long time, and I fear without a warm house, he will not survive the night," the man sadly said.

Salem smiled a peaceful smile at the man and responded, "I have plenty of wood for your use. Would you also like my help in building your house?"

The man looked excited and said, "Thank you, sir. You are too kind."

The two men spent the rest of the afternoon building the house. Salem also found some fuzzy-looking weeds to use as insulation inside the wall.

After the house was done, the man asked, "Is there anything that I can do for you?"

"No, just take care of your family," Salem said while thinking back to his life growing up.

He was poor, but his mama always had a meal and a roof over his head.

"I will, Your Majesty," the man said, and then he and his family disappeared.

"Was that my trial? That was extremely too easy," Salem bragged toward the sky. "Karisma, I thought this would be a hard trial."

A moment later, voices could be heard by the shore. Salem proudly walked to investigate the voices. As he made his way through the trees, in the direction of the shore, the voices grew louder, but Salem could not make out what was being said. Sounds of banging hammers could now be heard. Salem passed by the last tree and saw a large ship tied to a large dock.

"You made it back, Captain," a large sailor said.

The sailor stood over six feet tall and weighed close to three hundred pounds. His head was shaved bald, and he wore a patch over his left eye. His arms were enormous, muscular, and covered in tattoos. The giant skull stuck out to Salem more than the other small ones.

"Are"—Salem gulped—"are you talking to me?" he asked with fear in his voice.

"Methinks the captain had too much rum when he was gone. Yes, I am talking to you," the sailor said with a thundering chuckle.

Another sailor yelled, "Captain, the ship is ready to set sail. What be your orders?"

This sailor was a lot smaller than the other. He was around five feet tall and weighed around 125 pounds. Like the large man, he was also very muscular. Salem thought the men were strong because they all worked hard to sail a ship. This sailor wore no patch, and his hair was in a red and green Mohawk-style. His face had a large beard growing. He also wore three earrings in each ear.

Salem smiled and said, "Untie the ship, and let's set sail."

"Aye, aye, Captain," the crew yelled out.

Within a few moments, the ship was cut loose from the dock and sailing in open seawater. Salem was enjoying the open air. The fresh smell of salty sea water made Salem smile and long for more adventures.

About thirty minutes later, the large sailor, one that Salem believed was the first mate because he was the one that kept the men in order, bellowed out with his thunderous voice, "We should head to the south end of the island. There is a valuable treasure hidden near there. After we lay anchor in the south, it will be a few hours walk to the great treasure."

"What treasure is this?" questioned Salem, hoping for a chest full of gold.

"It is a flower"—everyone within an earshot of the word *flower* laughed—"that has many *magical properties*. It is said to give eternal

life, heal any wound, and also the ability to make you the most powerful man in the entire world," the first mate responded.

When he glared at the giggling crew, they all froze with fear.

"We should not get this flower," replied Salem, to the surprise of the entire crew. "That much power is too much for anyone to have."

"Captain," exclaimed the first mate and drawing his sword, "we will get that flower. If you don't want it, then *I* will have the great power it gives, and you shall meet your doom on the ocean's floor."

"Put your sword away. No one needs that power. With that much power, you can be tempted to do too much evil. It is not worth it," pleaded Salem.

The first mate swung his giant sword at Salem. Salem quickly ducked under the swing. Salem thought and wanted to tackle the first mate, but the size difference made it impossible. Salem took a chance and dove at the man's legs and held on for his life. The first mate kicked him off, and Salem dove at his legs again. This happened more than anyone could count on the ship. During the wrestling match, no one was manning the ship, and it ran aground. The jolt of the sudden stop knocked the sword out of the first mate's hand. Salem grabbed the massive sword with both hands and pointed it at the first mate's heart.

"This ends now. The flower will be left alone, and there will be no bloodshed on this ship." Salem looked at the smaller crew member and ordered, "Put this man in the brig."

Suddenly Salem appeared standing next to Goran facing the tower.

CHAPTER 21

Karisma Speaks, the Brothers Take Action

The brothers met in front of the tower. Karisma appeared in front of them, glowing with a blue mist and a giant smile on her face.

"Not all of you passed the trials," she spoke softly to them. "Each of you had to pass two parts to your trials. Two of you passed both parts of the trial. The third one of you did not pass the second test."

The brothers looked at each other in disbelief, each one thinking they passed their trials.

Karisma looked at Cass and said, "You first had to help a knight, a knight that once explored this island for Az Rex. He wanted a flower to heal himself, and you found another way to heal him by using your knowledge of plants. Cass, you also stood up to your brothers when they wanted help in retrieving the flower from the lake. You stood to your beliefs and did not give in to their pressure for the first time in your life."

Karisma spoke to Salem, "You found a family that needed help. You remembered your past and thought that your life wasn't as bad as it seemed. You used the resources in the forest for good and helped the family. Because of your help, the family could live comfortably for a long time. Your second trial, you overcame the temptation for greed and the lust for power. You faced difficult odds and found a way to win the fight without causing death or bloodshed. All these lessons are important as a king."

Salem replied, "Thank you."

Karisma glazed at Goran and said, "Goran, you first found a boy in the forest. You had a strong connection to this boy and helped him find long needed food and then helped him find his father. Your second trial, you met the boy once again. This time he was grown and trying to take care of his granddaughter, your great-great-granddaughter." Goran's heart felt like it stopped when he realized the boy was his son. Karisma continued, "The man begged and pleaded with his gold for you to obtain the flower for his granddaughter. You gave in to greed and took the gold to get the flower petal. You failed the trial and will not be a king on the island. You will go back to your poor life and not remember anything."

"Not remember anything?" Goran asked with eyes that wanted to be forgiven.

Karisma looked disappointed with him and said, "Nothing. You will not remember this island or your brothers. They will no longer be part of your life."

Karisma waved her hand, and Goran was gone, vanished into the thin air. Cass and Salem stood in shock at seeing their brother disappear into nothing.

Karisma looked tired and walked slowly into her tower. The door slowly shut with a loud thud, leaving Cass and Salem alone on the beach.

"What are we supposed to do?" asked Cass. Salem just shrugged his shoulders, still in disbelief. "We have to get Goran back. We always take care of each other. After all, he only got the flower petal to save the young girl, which turned out to be his great-great-granddaughter. To me, that means that he still has a place on the island because he took care of his family."

Salem shook his head in complete agreement and asked, "But how do we prove to Karisma that he did the right thing even though it was the wrong thing?"

The sun started to set, and the two boys set up a place to sleep on the shore of the lake. They did not sleep much, but instead, they talked about different ideas most of the night. They wanted Goran back so they could rule together like the old wizard foretold many years ago.

Karisma stared through her window off into the distance. She was deeply saddened that her brother could not pass the trial, even with her warnings. She just stood still looking out the window all night, watching the moon hanging over the lake.

Before dawn's light the next morning, the two boys ran off into the mountains to explore. They came to an open cleaning, one that looked like a city could be built on. Salem wondered if this was the spot where Goran had his first trial. The two agreed that this has to be the spot, so they investigated the area, hoping to find a mindless Goran wondering around. Unfortunately, they found nothing as they explored.

The boys were extremely frustrated but, not willing to give up, continued to think of what Karisma could have done with their lost brother. Cass looked out to the northern forest. It was a view that included the whole forest and the ocean that disappeared into the horizon. He noticed an island off the in the distance, an island that was not there when Karisma gave them the tour of their island. Cass pointed out the new island to Salem, and they both agreed Karisma had something to do with that, and hopefully that was where Goran was.

They quickly decided to make their way to the shore and find a way to get to the island. They made quick time getting down the mountain and through the forest, making it before nightfall. They made a camp and slept on the shore, excited but at the same time worried about the next morning.

Karisma decided to take a midnight flight, trying to clear her thoughts from the day. She circled around the island and noticed Salem and Cass sleeping by a dwindling fire. She blew a small fireball to relight the campfire. She saw that they seemed to be heading to the small island. Karisma's heart warmed; she waved her claw, and a small rowboat appeared on the shore, near where the boys were sleeping.

Karisma made her way back to her tower, hoping the boys could surprise her and force her to change her mind on Goran. She couldn't think of anything that would change her mind. He did break her one rule, but she was willing to see what they could come up with. Hope was restored to Karisma, and she hoped that it would help her brothers.

CHAPTER 22

The Mysterious Island

Cass woke up just as the sun started to peak the next morning. He stretched his arms, stood up, and looked at the sky, which was a blueish-orange color. It was a strange sight, but he didn't think much of it. He looked toward the ocean and saw the small lifeboat sitting on the shore, but he did not remember that sitting there the night before.

Cass looked down at a snoring Salem and kicked some sand over his face. The sand landed in his mouth and started to make Salem cough, which in turn woke him up. Salem, not looking happy about his wake-up, punched Cass in the chest, knocking him on flat on his back. After a few minutes of wrestling with each other, Cass finally pointed out the boat on the shore. The boys walked quickly to check it out.

The boat looked very seaworthy. It was made of cedar. No holes could be found, oars were inside and in perfect condition, and there was enough room for three people to fit.

"Shall we?" asked Cass.

"Yes, we shall set sail," replied a smiling Salem.

He was more than eager to find his brother, but also somewhat excited to sail the small part of the ocean.

They jumped in the boat at the same time. Salem pointed the error to Cass and made him get out and push the boat into the water.

Salem used the oar to help Cass. When the boat was finally moving in the water, Cass tried to jump in but landed face first into the water. He quickly jumped up, coughing up water through his nose. The sight of Cass made Salem tear up with laughter. After a few minutes of coughing, Cass finally got in the boat, and the journey to the mysterious island began.

The trip to the island was best described by Salem as "boring." Nothing happened. The few fish swam under the boat might have been the most excitement the boys had. The waves were small, and the current took them straight to the island. The trip took about thirty minutes.

Salem suggested they sail around the island to get an idea of where Goran might be. The island was almost shaped like a steep pyramid that rose straight out of the ocean. There was one small landing that they found. The landing had some broken wood sitting on it. The wood looked like a small smashed boat. Halfway up the cliff from the landing was a dark-looking cave that overlooked the open sea away from Karisma's island. Salem and Cass agreed that was the place that Goran would be. It looked like it would be a hard climb to the cave, but to save their brother the risk was worth it to them.

The climb was harder than it looked from the bottom. They reached the halfway point, and Salem thought about turning around and going home. Cass reminded him of how he was saved by Goran when he was arrested by the guard in the saloon.

"Brothers stick together," Cass sternly said, "and according to Karisma, you are supposed to be the brave one."

Salem, looking perturbed, said, "If we weren't on a cliff, you'd get it."

The rest of the way up to the cave was silent and slow. Eventually, they made it. Cass shook his arms, trying to regain feeling in his hands and fingers. Salem took a few deep breaths, trying to rest a moment.

"Who goes there?" was heard from the cave in an old scared voice.

Salem and Cass looked inside, seeing a skinny figure walking toward them. The person looked like Goran, but he was almost all bone. His hair was long and matted. His beard was halfway down his chest.

"Goran?" slowly asked Cass.

The man answered, "I was once called Goran. I haven't heard that name in many years ever since I left to seek my fortune overseas, and my boat slammed into the rocky shore of this island."

"Many years? You left us yesterday," Cass confusingly said. "Karisma sent you here as a punishment, and we just found you."

"We? I don't know you. I have never seen both of you. Who is Karisma? I have been on this island more years than I can remember," replied Goran.

Salem whispered to Cass, "I think Karisma erased his memories so we couldn't help him. There must be a way to make him remember."

Cass nodded in agreement, but he had no ideas how to help him.

"Goran, listen to me," pleaded Cass. "We are your brothers. We are triplets. We just found out that we were born as princes in a foreign country. Our older sister brought us to a magical island so we can rule the island together, as brothers, the three of us."

Goran said, "You have been drinking too much rum. I have no brothers, ever, and I don't believe in children's magical tails."

"You have to believe me," begged Cass. "Ask Salem. He will tell you."

"I don't think we can break Karisma's spell," Salem said with a blank look. "I am trying to think of what we can do, but I cannot think of anything."

Cass tearfully pleaded, "We cannot give up." He turned toward Goran, "What would make you believe me?"

"Nothing," replied Goran. "Now I have to go get my daily food. Every day for many years a fish appears in my fire. I am hungry."

"Wait, a fish appears in your fire every day? Your fire never goes out?" Cass cheerfully questioned.

"Yes. It makes hunting and gathering easy," said Goran. "I don't have to work for it."

Cass, finally smiling a bit after finding a way to get to Goran, said, "You don't believe in magic, but a fish appears to you every day, *magically*. Your fire never goes out, *magically*."

Goran, not wanting to listen, said, "Shut up. I am not listening to this anymore."

He walked up to Cass and shoved him out of the cave. Cass stepped back and slipped on the loose rocks and fell down the cliffs and landed with a giant thud.

Goran and Salem looked over the edge as Cass fell. Salem looked at Goran and was shocked at what he was seeing. Goran's appearance started to change. His hair was shrinking. His beard disappeared. His weight came back.

"We need to save Cass," screamed Goran.

"Welcome back, brother," said an unfazed Salem. "Let's go save another brother."

The trip down was a lot faster than the trip up. They reached Cass and saw that he was bleeding profusely from his head. It was bad. Goran took off his shirt and wrapped it around Cass's head.

Cass looked at Goran and said faintly, "I love you, brother." He took a very shallow breath and stopped breathing.

"We need to get to Karisma now," exclaimed a panicked Goran.

CHAPTER 23

Saving Cass?

Goran slowly picked Cass up over his shoulder and gently placed his lifeless body in the rowboat. Salem got in and grabbed an oar. Goran pushed the boat and jumped in and grabbed the other oar. Both boys started to paddle as fast as they could. Sweat started to drip from their faces. Goran wanted to save his brother, especially since he came to save him. Salem seemed extremely stunned at all that happened; he just stared silently at their island.

The silence was broken.

"I think we need to head to the sandy beach," Salem, who was choked up and trying to hold it back in his voice, said. "That would make the walking part of our journey easier."

"How are we going to move Cass when we get to the island?" asked Goran. "I can lift him, but carrying him that far is another matter."

Salem answered, "Honestly, I don't know. I have been thinking about making a sled out of the palm branches. I don't know if that would work, but I think we should give it a try. If you can think of anything better, please say it."

"That is a good idea. We can use the rope to pull him. We can take our time making it right so it will not fall apart during the journey. He is already dead, so time is something we do have," replied Goran.

Salem smacked Goran in the arm with the oar and said, "That wasn't very nice, but you do have a point."

The trip to the island took what felt like forever. The current was working against them, and the sun was starting to set as they reached the beach they left from earlier that morning. Unfortunately, they still had to row part way around the island to get to the sandy beach on the southern end of the island.

The moon started to rise. It was large, full, and it had a strange-looking blue coloring to it. Goran and Salem believed in their hearts that it was Karisma watching over them. Goran swore that he saw a dragon soar in front of the moon. He had a perfect view since the night was cloudless.

Goran looked up at the stars for the first time in his life and said, "This is what Cass is always looking at each night. It is more amazing than anyone could imagine. I didn't know there were so many stars in the sky."

Salem looked up and shook his head in agreement.

Salem guided the boat on the beach with ease because the moonlight made it easy to see. They left Cass's lifeless body in the lifeboat while they got to work on the palm branch sled. Both boys were exhausted when they finished at sunrise. They did not want to rest; their eagerness to save their brother kept their adrenaline high.

Goran carefully placed Cass in the center of the sled and said to Salem, "He looks so peaceful when he is dead."

"Don't you have any respect?" Salem reprimanded.

Goran seriously replied, "I said he looks peaceful."

Goran pulled the sled into the fields of weeds. That was easy, almost too easy. The sled performed perfectly, sliding over the weeds and grasses. Unfortunately, as they got to the forest, the sled got harder to pull. Both boys had to work together to pull the sled. There were a few times that Cass's head hit a tree or rock. There was one time when the sled got stuck in the mud and covered Cass's face. The worst was when the sled sank when they crossed the river. Cass's body sank with it, and Salem had to swim around to find Cass at the bottom of the river. These were stories that they agreed that Cass should never be told.

Eventually, they made it through the forest. Goran started to pull the sled up the mountain pass. Salem started to pull the sled toward the hot springs.

"What are you doing, Salem? We need to see Karisma. She can help us."

"Goran, Cass is dead. He has been dead for over a day. The magical flower is the only thing that can save him. He is beyond Karisma's help," forcefully argued Salem.

"You know the rule about the hot springs," Goran said loudly in a voice that echoes off the mountain pass.

Salem responded just as loud, "I want to save my brother, and you, or a rule, are not going to stop me."

Goran lowered his voice and peacefully said, "Look, Salem, I want to save my brother also. He never stopped believing he could save me. We always take care of each other. I know Karisma can save him."

"What do you suggest?" Salem humbly questioned.

Goran answered, "Go to Karisma. She will take care of Cass, trust me. I lost my trial because I saved a girl by getting the flower. I had many opportunities to stop, but I didn't. I believe Karisma would have helped if I just asked her for help. After Cass is saved, I will have to go on to face my punishment, and I don't want you to have the same fate as mine." Tears started to build in Goran's eyes as he looked down at Cass.

Salem looked at Goran and said, "You are right. I almost broke the rule that Karisma gave us because of my own greed to save my brother. I wasn't thinking about what the consequences would be. You have become wise, and I thank you for saving me."

The boys started to pull the sled up the pass, and a blue mist covered them. A quick moment later, they were at the tower. Goran and Salem were confused about what just occurred.

"What happened?" asked Cass, sounding like he just woke up from a nap.

Salem looked over toward in the sled, where Cass should be, and he was standing up, looking around.

"Why is Goran's dirty shirt tied on my head?" Cass asked.

"It is a long story. Perhaps I will tell you another day," Salem replied.

Karisma appeared before the three boys.

Goran gave Karisma a hug and whispered to her, "Thank you for saving Cass. I am sorry I shoved him over the cliff. It was all a huge accident. I am ready to go back to face my punishment. I am sorry I failed your tests."

Karisma smiled at Goran and said, "You just saved Salem from making the same mistake as you did. You and Salem saved Cass from death. You have earned your right to rule your kingdom on this island."

Goran looked shocked and surprised. He stood looking at Karisma and just nodded his head in agreement, not wanting to ruin the moment.

"I was dead?" Cass surprisingly asked. "What do you mean I was dead? You shoved me over a cliff?"

Salem looked at Cass, laughed, and said, "I told you it was a long story."

Karisma brightly smiled at the brothers and spoke kindly, "Well done. You three have earned your kingdoms. Cass, you will have the plains, and you will have the hot springs. The kingdom will be called Insidiaville because these plains are full of life. Use these plains to provide food for the island. Salem, you will have the forest in the north. You will call this kingdom Silvager because it is a great field of forests. The forest provides many resources for the island. Goran, you will have the mountains. This kingdom will be called Aurumton because it is full of gold. Use the gold to pay the people for their work, not for personal greed. You three will make cities in your kingdoms. You will also have the capital city in the center of the island, where all three kingdoms meet. This will be called Unidade, a city that will keep the island unified together."

CHAPTER 24

Kings of Their Land

"Why do we need have to have a city in the center of the island if we all have our own kingdoms?" asked Salem.

Karisma answered, "The city of Unidade will be the capital. You three will have your own kingdoms to watch over and rule, but you three will rule in the central city together. Doing this will keep the kingdoms at peace and the island as one."

Goran, deep in thought, asked, "We are three people. How are we each going to have a kingdom with no other people?"

"People will come," Karisma answered. "All of you will have families, and the island will be inhabited."

Karisma waved her hand, and the four of them vanished. A moment later, they appeared in the deep woods. A burned structure, which had the foundation of an old house, was in front of them.

"This is Unidade. This burned hut is where Ulrich, the great wizard of the wolf tribe, lived. Build a tomb around this sacred hut. This is a place of great importance to the island. This hut is where the magic of the island started. Rule wisely. Be just. Learn from each other. Take care of each other."

Karisma waved her hand again, and the four of them appeared on the southern sandy beach near the plains.

"Cass, this is where you build the capital city of your kingdom. Remember, your kingdom will supply food for the island. The fields will never stop bearing fruit as long as your kingdom does not fall into greed."

Karisma waved her hand a third time. This time the four appeared on the northern coastline, near the forest.

"Salem, your capital city will be built here. Use the resources of your kingdom to supply the people of the island. You have many natural resources that will be able to keep the island healthy. They will replenish themselves. Do not use your resources to gain power."

A fourth time, Karisma waved her hand. They all appeared in the clearing in the mountains.

"Goran, your capital city will be built here. Your kingdom is full of gold. Do not give into greed and lust for money, but use the gold to pay the miners. They will buy food and resources. This will spread the money around the island to the other kingdoms."

Once again, Karisma waved her hand. The four of them appeared at the hot springs.

"Cass, this is part of your kingdom. The water has magical properties. It can heal the sick. Use this wisely. Do not profit from this. All three of you, do not, under any circumstances, look for the flower in the springs. If you do this, your kingdoms will be gone *forever*."

Karisma waved her hands once more. Each one appeared back in their kingdom.

Karisma went back to her tower and looked at the setting sky and said, "Ulrich, I hope you know what you were doing."

A large blueish star twinkled and slowly fell through the sky.

The three boys had the same thoughts as they all appeared in their kingdoms. It was getting dark, and they were all alone. Cass gathered some weeds and made a fire. He found some crabs walking along the shore and caught them for dinner. Salem made a fire with some of the dried-up dead-wood from the forest. He caught a large rabbit and cooked that for his meal. Goran looked around and felt lost. He didn't have many trees but managed to find enough to start a small fire. He chased a heard of deer around, but failed to catch any of them. He did find a wild blueberry bush and had a small meal of fruit. The boys fell asleep, for the first time alone, but each in their own kingdom.

The next morning, Cass woke up before dawn and watched the sunrise over the ocean. A large ball of glowing orange slowly rose out of the ocean. The sky changed from black to purple to orange. In the distance, he spotted three large ships heading toward the island.

An hour later, the ships ran aground on the shore.

Cass greeted the people on the ships, "Welcome. I am Cass, a king of this land."

"Thank you," said an old-looking man. "We are people looking for a new place to settle. We have been treated poorly in our previous home, and we all left, hoping to find a new place to settle and start over. My ship is full of farmers and their families. The next ship is full of woodsmen and their families. The last ship is full of miners and their families. Would you like our services in your kingdom?"

"My kingdom is full of fresh and full fields that need to be farmed. I have two brothers, each a king in their own kingdoms. My brother Salem's kingdom is in the forest, and it is full of large trees and other resources. Goran, my other brother's kingdom, is in the gold-filled mountains. We all have work for you. Come with me. We will meet my brothers in Unidade, the capital city of the island. Sorry, the kingdoms are not built yet. We just became kings last night."

Cass and three shiploads of people walked to Unidade. The trip took a few hours, but everyone was happy and excited about their new homes. As Cass approached the city, his mouth dropped. Yesterday the city was nothing but a burned hut. Today a large and glorious castle stood tall. The castle looked like white marble and granite. It was trimmed in blue crystals. The main gate had a large wolf imprinted on it. The moat around the castle was the clearest water that Cass had ever seen. The clouds reflected perfectly. In the distance, Cass could see Goran coming from the mountains and Salem coming from the forest.

"Hello, brothers," Cass said. "It looks like Karisma left us a gift."

Goran, looking at the castle, just shook his head.

Salem said, "Yes, she did."

Cass asked, "How did you know to come here?"

Goran, with a rumbling stomach, replied, "I felt like I needed to be here. Something inside kept telling me to come here."

Salem said, "Me too. I felt like you needed me to be here."

"These people landed on the island this morning. They came in three ships. One was full of farmers. One was full of woodsmen. The last was full of miners. They want to know if they are welcome on the island and able to live in our kingdoms," Cass explained to his brothers.

"Yes," exclaimed Salem and Goran together.

Cass looked at the people and said, "This is my brother Salem. All of you people that are woodsmen, he will be your king. This is my brother Goran. He will be the king of the miners. The farmers will go with me. We are in the city of Unidade. This is the capital of the island. My brothers and I will rule together here at this castle."

Each of the new kings led their people to the location of their capital cities. Over the next few years, cities and castle were built. Roads and trails were made. Each kingdom prospered. Each king would fall in love, marry, and start a family of their own.

CHAPTER 25

The Prophecy Begins

The kingdoms continued to prosper over the next twenty years. Cass had two sons and two daughters. Goran had two sons and one daughter. Salem had one son. The three brothers ruled justly and with great honor from and Unidade and their kingdoms. The brothers decided to meet twice monthly in the capital city. Karisma never appeared to the brothers or to the people, but the three knew she was always watching over them.

Twenty or so more years passed. Like the previous twenty years, not much is known, other than the children had grown up and had families of their own. Salem's son had two sons of his own. The oldest, Gerald, was to take over the kingdom when Salem was gone. Goran's oldest and firstborn son had two sons also. His oldest was Than. Cass's oldest son had three sons. The youngest was Rider.

Rider became a great farmer, perhaps the greatest of all on the island. He was taller than Cass. He had the same dark eyes of his grandfather, and his curly, dark hair grew down his back. He would grow larger crops than anyone. He would pay the workers of his fields greatly. He would even charge less money for people to buy his crops. The island's people loved him. The people of Insidiaville wanted him to be the next king, but since he was the youngest of his brothers, that was not to be.

Than was known for his great strength and explosive temper. He stood over eight feet tall and was the size of an ox. His light-brown hair and beard looked like a lion's mane. He boasted greatly how he fought and killed two bears at one time, one bear with each hand. He was also known for cheating people. He would keep some of the miners' wages for his own pockets. He would cheat the scales when buying food. Stories started to spread about him stealing from people, but the people who told the stories disappeared and would never be seen again. People of the island feared Than.

Than made his weekly trip down to Insidiaville so he could buy his weekly food. People turned the other direction when they saw him coming.

A loud voice thundered, "You, stop. Come and sell me your crops."

"M-m-m-m-me?" answered the man.

"Yes. Get over here now," Than's voice echoed.

Than bought all the man had to offer but only paid a fourth of the asking price.

"My dad is a king. I am not going to pay your prices," Than would boast as he left.

Rider saw what Than did to the man that day and confronted him outside the city.

"Why did you steal from that man?"

"Get out of my way, you inferior prince. I can do what I want, and no one can stop me. Not even you or your grandfather. They will be gone soon, and I will be the new king. You will bow to me. I am bigger and stronger, and no one can stop me. I fought two bears and killed them both. You could not hurt that worm on the ground," Than boasted loudly.

Rider corrected, "This is not what our grandfathers taught us. They rule with great honor, something they want us to do."

Than roared, "Away from me, you maggot."

Than looked at Rider and shoved him. Rider fell back next to his ax. As Than walked away, Rider picked up the ax and flung it toward Than, striking him in the back of the head. Than fell face-down and landed with a great thud. Rider ran to the divot that Than caused when he landed.

"I am sorry," he said over and over.

Than tried to pull himself up, but he failed. He died moments later in the middle of the road.

Rider quickly grabbed his ax and ran to his grandfather's castle. He told Cass everything. Cass had some of the men go and retrieve Than's body. Cass thought they should hide the body and never speak of the story. It was decided that the body would be tossed into the ocean and held down with some anchors. That way no one could find it, ever.

That night a ship left the shore and sailed out a few miles, dropped the body into the depths of the sea, and then came back to the docks. Cass was given the news. Each man was ordered to never speak of the events that night.

The next day Cass was to travel to Unidade to meet with his brothers. Cass left at his usual time and arrived at the same time his brothers got there. They gave each other the usual greeting and left to meet and discuss the business of the island.

As they were walking to the meeting room, Goran asked, "Has anyone seen Than? He never came home yesterday. The last time anyone saw him was before he left on his weekly trip to buy food in the market at Insidiaville."

Cass and Salem both answered, "We have not seen him."

Goran said, "I sent some guards to look for him, but their search has turned up nothing. They will continue their search until they find him. Knowing Than, he probably stopped to fight a bear or something."

The meeting lasted through the night, and each brother returned to their castle the next day.

During the meeting, Rider became filled with guilt. He wanted to tell someone what happened, but he did not know who to talk with. He looked toward the mountains and cried. A glowing blue object appeared over the mountains and came toward Rider. He felt a great fear inside as the shape came closer and closer. The glowing blue cloud shape landed next to him and changed into a lady.

"I am Karisma. I believe that we need to talk."

Through the night, Rider and Karisma talked about the past events. Rider told Karisma how he was scared because his grandfather never hid anything before.

Before Karisma left, she tearfully said, "Murder, even though it might be just, is still a murder. The island has been tainted. This is the start of the island's fall. The prophecy has begun."

The next day Karisma appeared to Cass on the way home from the meeting in Unidade.

"Karisma!" exclaimed Cass. "I have missed seeing you."

"How is everything going? Is there any news that you would like to tell me?" cautiously questioned Karisma.

"Everything is great," Cass answered. "The island is prospering, and the people are happy. The new city of Sonoma is almost complete."

"How are your brothers? Did Goran find what he was looking for?" Karisma questioned without being too obvious she knew the events that transpired.

Trying to hide the fear in his heart, Cass responded, "They are doing well. I didn't know that Goran was looking for anything."

Karisma left after saying her goodbyes and returned to her tower. Cass made it back to his palace in Insidiaville, wondering how much Karisma knew and how she might have learned of what happened.

Karisma spent the night in meditation and talking to herself and Ulric.

"How can this happen?" she blamed Ulric.

"It was only a matter of time before greed and corruption would take over," Ulric answered with a thunderous voice from the sky. "Remember the prophecy. Four generations must pass, then the child will lead this island back together. Things will get worse. Brother will turn on brother. Greed and the lust for power will take over, except for the one who lost a son today. He will be the rock of the island. His kingdom will be solid. His offspring will lead this island back to one. Hair of gold, eyes of blue, will be your sign." The voice faded, and Karisma cried for Goran's loss.

Cass summoned Rider the next morning. The two planned on meeting near the palace, but Rider never showed. Cass became angry and left to find Rider.

Karisma quietly appeared to Cass while he was searching for Rider.

"Rider is sleeping. He will not be harmed," she said to a startled Cass. "He is under my protection."

"Why would he need your protection?" asked Cass.

"I know your intentions. You fear the information he has. The same information he shared with me," Karisma sternly said.

A surprised Cass forcefully questioned, "He told you? That is what I thought. He was told *not* to say anything to anyone."

"I already knew what happened. He told me the truth, unlike what you have done. You lied to me, and you lied to your *own* brother. When does the lying stop?" Karisma said in a scolding and hurtful tone.

"I, I, I, I don't know. I am going to Goran now," Cass fearfully said.

Karisma comforted Cass, "Very good. He will not harm you, I promise you that. Go and make things right with your brother."

The two parted company, and Cass hurried to Aurumton to see his brother.

CHAPTER 26

The Sad Loss of Than

Cass made his way quickly to see Goran. He thought about the events that happened and how he could fix what happened. He did not know how to fix it, but he was sure that Karisma was right that he would not be harmed.

The path through the mountains was harder than Cass remembered, and it seemed to take forever; but after a few hours, Cass was at Aurumton City, the location of Goran's palace.

The people in Aurumton City knew who Cass was, and it was not long before he was with his brother in the massive courtyard.

Cass bowed his head down and spoke in a soft tone, "I am sorry, my brother."

Goran looked surprised, "Sorry for what?"

Cass spent the next hour telling Goran the story of what happened between Rider and Than. He told of how the body was hidden at sea. He also told Goran of his meeting with Karisma.

"I came here for your forgiveness. I will do anything you ask to make up for the harm that my family and I caused to you."

"You cannot make up for a life," Goran exclaimed. He looked at Cass with angry eyes. Cass looked up at Goran with tears in his eyes. "I will not harm you, but you will have to make this up to my family. We lost a big piece of the family, and we will not be able to make that up. I know he was headstrong and had his problems, but deep down his heart was larger than he was. Come with me, and I will show you."

Goran led Cass to the back side of the palace, where the stables were located.

"You see that child next to the horse?" asked Goran.

"Yes, I do," replied Cass. "I didn't know that he has children."

"He doesn't. This child was left orphaned. His mother passed away during childbirth, and his father was killed in a mine collapse when he was three. This child was left with nothing. Than saw him and took him in as his own son. He loved this child more than anything."

Goran took Cass to the mines and said, "All these miners loved when Than came by here. Than would use his enormous strength to break the rock that they couldn't. He also brought them food. It is hard work being a miner. I tried it for a day, and it is something that I never want to do again."

Goran took Cass into the palace and showed him the library.

"Than, as much of a giant he was, loved to read. He could quote almost every book in here from his memory. He would go to the town center and resight books for the people. Most of the town's people cannot read, and Than was their way to enjoy a book. He had different voices for each character and would act out the book."

"I never knew Than was like this. I always saw him as a brute and a giant. Why would he not want to pay for the food he bought each week?" asked Cass.

"That I do not know. I wish I could answer that. I wish you would have talked to me about that. I would like to think it was for a greater good, one that I will never know about him," sadly answered Goran.

"Please let me talk with the boy. I need to let him know what happened and also let him know that he will be taken care of," begged Cass.

Cass spent the rest of the day with the boy. Cass reassured him that he would be taken care of. He and Goran would not let anything happen to him, ever.

Cass went back to Goran that evening. Goran packed some supplies for Cass.

"I have a way for you to make up the loss," Goran said.

Cass asked, "What would that be?"

"Send Rider here to work the mines for one year. Let him get to know the men who work hard. Let him experience the backbreaking work. That will repay the debt of the loss of Than," Goran replied.

Cass made the trip back to Insidiaville and began to search for Rider. He sent out a unit of soldiers from his army to search throughout the night and the next day.

Rider, after talking with Cass, decided that he did not want to work the mines and headed north to Silvager. He wanted to get as far away from Insidiaville and the murder of Than as fast as he could. He hoped that he could catch a ship and get off the island.

He made his way to the outskirts of Tilton, the capital of Silvager.

Suddenly he heard a quiet voice, "Come here, boy."

"Who are you?" asked Rider while looking around.

"I know who you are and what you have done. You need to pay for your crime," the voice echoed.

"Wh-wha-wha-what crime?" asked Rider.

"The murder of Than," echoed throughout the forest.

An arrow flew from the trees and struck Rider in his stomach. Rider fell to his knees.

A man ran through the trees and yelled, "He is down, take all that he has." Three more men ran out and robbed Rider of everything he had. They left him to die on the road. "That is one less murderer we have to worry about," the man boasted.

All the men left, and Rider looked up at the sky. He was too weak to move.

"I am sorry for everything I have done," he said as he took his final breath.

A wolf, glowing with a blue cloud, sat down next to him and howled into the night, as if it was crying to the moon. The wolf grabbed Rider's body gently in his mouth and leaped toward the sky. The wolf vanished into thin air, along with the body of Rider.

The soldiers reported back to Cass, telling him that Rider was nowhere to be found. The mystery of Rider haunted Cass for the rest of his life. Goran told Cass over and over that he knew nothing. Cass never believed him. Salem kept quiet on all the events that took place. He just wanted to keep the peace between the kingdoms.

CHAPTER 27

The End of the Brothers

For sixty years, the brothers ruled over their kingdoms and ruled over the whole island. Their families grew, and the island prospered. The magic remained strong, and Karisma was mostly happy with all she saw.

Cass died first. Karisma made a tomb over the ashes of Ulric's hut. Cass was laid to rest in the rightmost grave. The orphaned boy from many years ago gave a speech for his adopted father, thanking him for what he had done for him.

Goran died a week later, leaving a large hole in the hearts of Aurumton. The miners placed lit candles in the mines the night he died in honor of their king. He was laid to rest in the center grave of the tomb.

A month later, Salem took his last breath. On his deathbed, he told his son a story about how he had Rider robbed to teach him a lesson, but the men took it too far and killed him. He held the secret for many years, and it ate him up inside, not being able to tell the truth of what happened. He was supposed to keep the peace, but he had no peace in his heart. He was laid to rest to the left of Goran.

Each king had their kin in place to take over their reign. Soon after the new kings took control, the city of Unidade became empty. Soon it became a forgotten ruin with the king's tomb. The new kings and queens did not want to rule with each other; they just wanted to rule their own kingdom. Each generation wanted more power and more control. The lust for power changed the island. It started to lose its magic, and Karisma went into hiding.

Before Karisma went into hiding, she wrote down the prophecy of Ulric.

> *The island will become corrupt*
> *after the passing of the three.*
> *The people will kill.*
> *Four generations will pass.*
> *A girl will be born,*
> *one with hair of gold*
> *and eyes of the sky;*
> *will find the magic*
> *and restore the island.*

Karisma cast a spell on herself, one to make her sleep until the time comes when the girl will find the magic. Her spirit would watch over the girl until the time was right.

PART III

The Next Generation

Eighty years passed since the death of the three brothers. Aurumton was a very peaceful kingdom. The king and queen, Edward and Isabel, had one child, a beautiful daughter named Nicola, a girl with long golden-blonde hair, which flowed halfway down her back and waved in the breeze. She had the most beautiful sky-blue eyes. Nicola was told that the golden hair came from the gold in the mountains, and her eyes were a reminder of the heavens. She stood just below average and was a girl of an average build with lightly tanned skin, but her beauty was as great as her kingdom. She developed a strange accent, one that no one could figure out how she got it. If you combined American Southern English and Australian together, that was how the accent would sound. She was not known for her proper manners, and she could burp with the largest of men, but all the people on the island adored her anyway. She would often fight with her parents on dressing formal, something she hated. If she had her choice, she would just wear her plain white riding clothes with her brown leather boots. Nicola was also a skilled swordswoman and could battle any of the royal guards. She loved nothing more than the outdoors and just enjoying the simple things.

Insidiaville, once a great farming kingdom, was now a vast desert region, with few natural resources to call their own. However, one city, Desert Springs, had natural springs that bubbled up fresh, sweet-tasting water. The water was said to have magical properties, including the ability to heal the sick. People would come from all around the island to drink the magical spring water. The king and queen, William and Helen, of Insidiaville also had a son named Caelon. He was short, standing just below five feet and heavy-set. He had short and curly red hair and light-green eyes. His face was freckled, and his skin was a pasty white. He spoke like he was from Scotland. No one understood how that came to be, except he did visit Scotland for a week when he was two. He always wore the Insidiaville formal clothing, forest-green pants and tunic that were laced with gold tassels in the shape of wheat. He wore the prince's crown at all times so he could remind the people who he was. Caelon was four years older than Nicola, but when he was twenty-two and on Nicola's eighteenth birthday, they were married for Insidiaville's political gain. Even with the political gain, Caelon loved being the center of attention, but would never do anything that wasn't a certain guarantee. If he had any kind of doubts or if he wasn't strong enough, there was always someone to be manipulated to do the job.

The kingdom of Silvager was still extremely rich in forests and other natural resources. The kingdom of Silvager was more advanced than the other kingdoms on the island. The people there had developed guns instead of the bow and arrows used in the other two kingdoms. The guns were close to what have been used in the American Revolution. They had better and faster chariots along with better ships for the sea. Silvager was now known for its pirates and had long held the port of Facultas, the capital of Insidiaville, under siege. However, even with all these advantages, tragedies could happen. The king and queen, Louis and Amanda, were enjoying a vacation and were lost at sea. With the whole kingdom in mourning, Tero, their son, the prince of Silvager, was getting ready to accept the crown to become the new king. He was known as a great warrior. He was very strong and muscular and stood over six and a half feet. He had deep dark-brown eyes and short, wavy black hair. He was very educated when he spoke and sounded almost British. He would wear black pants and a black shirt under his silver armor. The royal flag was imprinted on the right shoulder of his armor. He always had his silver sword, with a black gold handle, at his side. He was twenty-one, and according to Silvagerian tradition, he would choose a wife. All the ladies in the kingdom hoped that he would choose them to be his wife.

The island was in mourning for the loss of Louis and Amanda but excited to see Tero became the new king.

CHAPTER 28

The Crowning of Tero

Tero looked out of the balcony window toward the gathering crowd.

"I am *ready* to be the king," he exclaimed to his most trusted advisor, Eldred. "The opportunity is upon me. This is an opportunity that I will not waste, one that my parents wasted. They were weak, and I will rule with an iron fist. Nothing will ever again stop this kingdom from progressing forward."

Eldred, wearing the silver-lined, black Silvager royal inauguration robes, asked, "What do you mean, wasted?"

Tero answered, "They never did anything to help move the kingdom forward. They were content with what they had, not what they could have. I deserve more, and so does this crown." Tero's eyes stared toward the jewel-filled crown that would soon be his.

"What do you want?" asked Eldred.

"First, I want Nicola, the princess of Aurumton and Insidiaville, as my queen," quickly answered Tero.

"You know she is married to Caelon, the prince of Insidiaville," Eldred answered.

"I know. Caelon is not worthy of the crown of his own kingdom. Better yet, he is not worthy to be married to a lady of such beauty. He is the biggest idiot on this island. His bride has such great beauty and power, but he won't even *touch* her. She has slept every night in her own castle, alone, waiting for a real king."

"How will you take her as your wife when she is already married?" seriously questioned Eldred.

A large smirk appeared on Tero's face, and he said, "An opportunity will arise."

A loud knock on the door was heard.

"Who knocks?" loudly asked Eldred.

"The first mate from the king and queen's shipwreck is awake and wishes to speak to you," the booming voice from behind the door said.

"Bring him in," ordered Tero.

A weak and scruffy-looking man was brought into the room. With fear in his eyes, he looked toward Tero.

"What news do you have that would interrupt my day of glory?" asked Tero.

The sailor answered, "Th-th-the." He cleared his throat and continued, "The shipwreck was not an accident in bad weather, as you might have heard. The ship was attacked. The seas were smooth, and the sun was shining brightly. We never saw the flag of the ship that attacked us. The attack was swift, and somehow only I survived."

Tero, with his eyes and voice filling with fear and anger, asked, "How did you survive and not protect my parents, the king and queen?"

"An explosion knocked me away from the wheel, and I landed on a piece of the ship which was floating on the water. I was very lucky. I then drifted for many days, so many days. One of your attack boats on the way back from Insidiaville picked me up and brought me back. I don't know how many days it has been," the sailor weakly replied.

Eldred looked at Tero and then at the crowd outside and said, "It is time to start the coronation."

Eldred opened the door and greeted the excited crowd.

Tero addressed the guard quietly, "Take this sailor to the dungeon. When you get there, kill him. If Eldred asks, tell him that he died of his injuries. Dump his body in the bay and never speak of what you heard. I don't want this news of an attack getting out. The news would hurt our chances of our great kingdom progressing where I want it to."

"As you command," the guard said, turning around and taking the sailor with him.

As Eldred spoke loudly to the crowd, he raised his right hand toward the sky, the sign that it was time for Tero to join him. Tero walked on the balcony and was greeted with a resounding cheer. Eldred took the crown in his left hand and placed it on Tero's head. The cheer became louder.

"I present your new king, King Tero," Eldred screamed toward the crowd.

Tero waved his hand at the crowd, and the crowd quieted down.

"Thank you, Eldred. Thank you, people of Silvager. Today will be remembered forever as a day of change and progression. I will take every opportunity to make this noble kingdom grander. I will not stop at anything."

The crowd cheered, and Tero turned around and proudly walked back into the room.

"I am glad that is over," Tero said to anyone that was listening.

Eldred followed Tero and said, "That was short and to the point."

Tero smiled, "The way I like it. The rest of this island will get my message soon enough."

A messenger came into the room and said, "Your Majesty, I have a message from Caelon. He wishes to meet with you in two days."

"What does this meeting include?" questioned Tero, sensing a great opportunity just arose.

"I don't know. There was no information given to me. Caelon just told me to set up a meeting in two days," answered the messenger.

"Tell Caelon that I will be there in three days. If it is important, he will wait the extra day. Eldred, get this man some food and some better-looking clothes. The Insidiaville green makes me sick to my stomach."

Trying his best to keep a straight face, Eldred responded, "Yes, Your Majesty."

Three days later, Tero made his way to Insidiaville to meet with Caelon.

CHAPTER 29

The Road to Sonoma

One week later, a lone and young female traveler rode from Aurumton City, the capital of Aurumton, to Aurumton's southern city of Sonoma. Aurumton was known for their gold, not their originality. The warm spring morning was full of vibrant color. The bright orange sun was rising in the east. The birds were chirping loudly, awaking the full smell of spring.

A unit of three royal guards from Insidiaville and a single prisoner, who was being transported to the city of Desert Springs for a trial, was waiting on a hill about the halfway point on the road to Sonoma. The road followed the Aurumton River, which was the dividing line between the two kingdoms of Aurumton and Insidiaville. The river, which was full of life, peacefully flowed south. The east side of the river, where the dirt road was located, was in a full dense forest with foothills starting to climb eastward toward the Aurumton Mountains. The west side of the river marked the beginning of the vast desert of Insidiaville. The desert had evidence of former fields, long rock walls in straight lines could be seen for miles, but those fields had long dried up. The guards positioned themselves on a hill that was sticking up just above the tree line.

"We need to stop this lady from reaching Sonoma. That is the direct order from Prince Caelon," the captain of the unit said. "Load the catapult and get ready to fire."

The captain wore the Insidiaville formal military uniform. The uniform consisted of forest-green pants and a forest-green tunic, black leather boots, bronze shoulder padding, iron gloves, and an iron helmet, which he kept the shield up so he could have a perfect vision of his target.

"Are you sure that she is our target?" the first guard asked. His uniform was not as formal. He did not have the shoulder pads, and his pants had to be stitched together a few times.

"A lone female traveler with long, dark hair riding a white horse with brown ears and a brown tail on the road next to the river—she is everything that Caelon said. Yes, she is the target," the captain confirmed. "Remember, there are repercussions for questioning your commander. I don't want to punish you again."

"Sir, we are out of stones for the catapult," the first guard said with some nervous squeaking in his voice.

"What? How did that happen? You had one job, and that was to make sure we have the stones loaded and that they are ready to be used," the captain said with a very large concern building in his voice.

"Yes, sir," the guard nervously said. "I loaded ten stones. There are the ropes I used to secure them. The ropes look like they have been tampered with. There are some cuts marks on them.

"We have to stop her." The captain looked around the area. "Use the prisoner in place of the stone. This will make our job easier at the end of the day. We won't have to transport him to Desert Springs, plus there will be no need for a trial," ordered the captain, trying to sound smart. "We get to do the execution now. I believe he was *trying* to escape."

The second guard, who was large and pale, dressing in just raggedy forest green pants and no shirt because no one could ever find one that fit him, smirked at this command and reached for the large potato sack that was in the carriage. He grabbed the half-conscious prisoner, tied him into a ball, and then stuffed him into the potato sack. The guard tied the sack, and then he loaded the makeshift ammunition into the catapult and then waited for the command to fire at the unsuspecting traveler.

A few quiet moments passed, then...

"*Fire!*" yelled the captain, and the prisoner was hurled toward the dirt road below.

At the moment of launch, the prisoner came to his senses, not knowing what was going on, but he felt a strange sensation, something like he was flying…then *smack*, he felt something firm. The traveler, on her way to Sonoma with an urgent message from the king of Aurumton, was knocked off her horse and sent flying across the path and rolled until she splashed into the river.

Seeing their job was complete, the guards turned back and headed home to make a full report to Tero on the events that transpired this morning.

The traveler swam back to the river bank, confused and trying to figure out what just hit her. When she got back to the trail, she found the horse had a broken leg and would not be able to continue the journey. She also found a potato sack with a human hand sticking out. Faint moaning was heard from inside the sack. She slowly made her way to the sack to look inside. To her surprise, when the sack was untied, a dazed man was inside. The traveler untied the man and pulled him out of the sack. She made her way back to the river to get some water to splash on the man's face.

The man, starting to regain his senses, looked up at the girl and said with a confused look, "Why are you wearing a wig?"

Embarrassed, she grabbed her hair to find the dark-haired wig was half off her head, showing her golden-blonde hair.

She blushed and said, "I am delivering an urgent message from the king and queen to the city of Sonoma, and I need to get there quickly. The disguise is supposed to keep people from recognizing me."

"Well, unfortunately, you are not going to get there quickly now," said the man as he made note of the injured horse. "What is your name? Your real name. Not your dark-haired, wig-wearing alter ego."

She looked at the man, her face turning red with some slight anger, and reluctantly answered, "Nicola…"

"Aren't you the—" the man started to say.

"The princess of Aurumton", Nicola annoyingly interrupted.

With a smile, the man replied, "Nice to meet you, Your Highness. I am Fitzpatrick, but you can call me Fitz, and I have a message for you. I was on my way to Aurumton City when I was captured by Caelon's guards."

"Oh, really? And by chance, you flew into my horse," Nicola questioned with a slight attitude.

"Yes, and I overheard a secret meeting between your husband"—Nicola rolled her eyes at the sound of that—"and Tero, the new king of Silvager, about a plot to kill your parents and take over your kingdom."

"Why would the kingdom of Silvager, our loyal friends and allies for many years, want to help Insidiaville and *my husband*, Caelon? Silvager has always been fighting the power-hungry Insidiaville."

Fitz answered, "Caelon wants the gold of your kingdom, and he needs the advanced weaponry of Silvager to succeed in his mission."

"Tero wouldn't give in to these demands because he needs our gold to pay for his country. But still, if Caelon wants to kill my parents? This is disturbing. If he succeeds in killing them, he will not stop," Nicola said with some concern growing.

Fitz, trying to keep Nicola calm, answered, "You are right. It is all about the power and gold. He wants more than he deserves. I have given you my message. Let's see about getting your message to Sonoma. I will help you in getting there. We will have to walk the rest of the way. There is no way the horse is going anywhere. Unfortunately, we will not make it before tomorrow, and these roads are not safe at night. I will protect you, Your Majesty."

"I still have one question for you. When is this evil plot going to be carried out? How much time do we have?" asked Nicola.

"His plan is to be carried out on your first anniversary in four weeks," answered Fitz.

"That day is also my nineteenth birthday. The whole kingdom is going to be there for a celebration. That would make a bold and mighty statement to the whole island having the king and queen murdered on that day," Nicola concluded, stifling her fear.

CHAPTER 30

Caelon's Plan

Before Nicola and Fitzpatrick left for the journey ahead, Fitz walked down to the river to clean himself up. He took off his tattered black shirt and examined his shoulder, which was still throbbing from the sudden impact into the horse. He was hurting but did not want to show Nicola that. Nicola looked over at Fitz, and it did not take her long to notice that Fitz was a tall, around six feet tall, with a dark tan. His medium-length black hair waved down his neck. His eyes were very dark and large. He was also very muscular. He was twenty years old, just about a year older than Nicola. She wanted to keep looking but not get caught staring. Fitz put his shirt back on and started walking back to the road. He smiled and watched Nicola as he made his way back.

"What are you staring at?" Nicola said with an amused smile on her face.

"Um, nothing. Just thinking about what happened today."

As Fitz said this, the two began their walk to Sonoma. The trip normally would take a few hours, but with unexpected delays and nightfall coming in a few hours, travel would be slower. Still, they expected to reach Sonoma by midmorning the next day.

As the two walked, Nicola broke the ice by asking, "So how did you get captured, and what was with the potato sack?"

"Do you really want to know?" Fitz answered reluctantly. He looked behind them. "Stay here. I think I heard a noise behind us. Let me check it out." A few minutes later, Fitz returned. "I was wrong, it was nothing."

"Okay," Nicola said, waiting patiently for Fitz to return. When he did get back, she asked with a hint of amusement in her voice, "Now, I would love to hear the story of what got you captured."

"Well, it all started when I was traveling through the city of Facultas, the capital of Insidiaville—"

"I know that. My husband's palace is there," interrupted a sarcastic-sounding Nicola.

"I saw Caelon, your husband—" Fitz said, cutting Nicola off from her interruption by placing his finger on her lips.

Nicola, wanting to get the last word in, pushed Fitz's finger away and interrupted again, "I know who he is. I have met him a few times—"

Fitz kept talking over Nicola's voice, continuing where he left off, "Walking with Tero, the newly crowned king of Silvager. Knowing the violent history of the two countries, I had some curiosity, and I followed them at a distance, but close enough to overhear what was being said."

"Apparently you were seen," Nicola quickly interrupted again.

"I was getting to that part, and if you let me finish, I will tell you," Fitz said while waiting for Nicola's approval. With a nod of her head, he calmly continued, "The two made their way to a tavern near the center of the city. I stayed close enough to them to overhear their conversation—"

"'Why do you, Caelon, the lowly and cowardly prince of Insidiaville, want to meet with a powerful king, like me?' Tero asked.

"Caelon glared and answered, 'First of all, a 'hello' would do, and secondly, my condolences to you and your kingdom for the loss of your parents, and congratulations on your coronation. I know our countries have had many differences in the past, and I am willing to look past those and make way for peace between our great and noble kingdoms. All I ask is that you help me in achieving my ultimate plan.'

"'And, what plan would this be?' asked Tero while he was annoyingly tapping his fingers on the table to see if Caelon would get frustrated.

"'I want to conquer Aurumton, something my grandfather started many years ago. It is something I want to complete. I want the gold and the power that comes with it. My parents wanted peace, against my grandfather's wishes, but I will complete his great conquest,' Caelon replied while looking at Tero's tapping fingers.

"'What do you need from Silvager?' questioned Tero while listening to Caelon intently.

"Caelon replied with all sincerity, 'I need your advanced weaponry to destroy Aurumton.'

"Tero smugly laughed, saying, 'They are not for you to use. We used our resources and advanced technology to make these weapons. Your country has nothing except dirt, and furthermore, your army could never learn how to use them.'

"'I will pay you greatly for them,' Caelon said, almost starting to beg.

"Tero, in a stern tone, said, 'Payment? Okay, we will take half of the gold from Aurumton for the use of my weapons.'

"Caelon, in a small fit of rage, said, '*Ha*, there is not a chance you will get that much gold. I will give you 20 percent of all the gold.'

"Tero slammed his fist down and sternly replied, 'Do not test me! You know what happens to your ships at sea. You know we control the shipping routes. We will continue to capture and sink all of your ships. Your 20 percent offer means nothing to Silvager. 50 percent will allow you to have control over your seaport once again and freedom from Silvager's pirates.'

"Caelon's face burned red with anger at this offer and said, '30 percent, and that is my final offer.'

"'Thirty percent will work, but as you know, my pirates cannot be controlled,' Tero teased arrogantly.

"Caelon took a few deep breaths and continued in a calmer tone, 'In four weeks Nicola and I will celebrate our first wedding anniversary and also her nineteenth birthday. The king and queen are throwing a kingdom-wide celebration, and my parents will also be there to join in the festivities. The plan starts with the execution of my parents, then the king and queen of Aurumton. Next, my army will invade and crush the city, with the whole country at the celebration. Thereupon, my rule will begin.'

"'What would your wife say about the murder of her parents? You know how much all the people love her and how they listen to everything she says. She is the backbone of Aurumton, and your country's people, along with my country's people, are in love with her.' questioned Tero while starting to plot ideas in his head.

"Caelon angrily replied, 'I don't care what she thinks. She has been a pawn in this plot since her parents and mine agreed to the wedding in the name of "peace." I have never loved or touched her, and I never will. The golden-blonde hair makes me sick. I am tired of hearing how the heavens made her eyes and how her hair is like the gold of the mountains. It is a sign of weakness that the people love her. Power comes from fear. Her arrogance and beauty make it impossible to have any kind of power over the people. She will soon learn the true meaning of power! Nicola will obtain some information later today about an upcoming attack on the city of Sonoma from the city of Desert Springs. With this information, she will want to tell her uncle, the governor of Sonoma, the news herself. She will put on her disguise, a black wig, and begin the journey. During this journey, I will have her murdered—'"

"You did not think to tell me that part of the plot first?" again Nicola interrupted.

Fitz smiled at her, placed his hand over her mouth, and kept telling the story.

"—'On the way to Sonoma, my royal guards will have their catapult ready so they can kill her.'"

"After Caelon said that, I moved slightly and a glass fell over and shattered on the floor. This is when the two princes looked at me. Caelon yelled, 'Capture him! He has heard the whole plan and must be stopped.' I ran out as fast as I could with a unit of three guards chasing me. I made it through most of the city until I turned down a dead-end street. The last thing I remember was a club hitting me in the head. The next thing I knew I was flying into a horse and knocking a beautiful lady into the river."

"Stop that. You are making me blush." Fitz smiled at Nicola to make her blush more. "My clothes are still damp. I am starting to get cold. We should stop here and make a fire so we can stay warm tonight."

"Let's gather some dry wood. I will start the fire," Fitz replied as he immediately started to work on the fire.

Ten minutes later, a raging campfire was burning. Both of the travelers relaxed and tried to get some sleep when the sunset through the trees, but Fitz kept hearing noises in the forest. He would check out each noise, but nothing ever came of them.

CHAPTER 31

Sonoma

Nicola was awakened by the sound of Blue Vangas singing their morning song. She looked around and saw that Fitz was gone. She didn't think much of it, thinking he left sometime in the night. A few minutes later, she got up and walked down to the river to wash her face so she could wake herself up a little more. She put her wig back on as she would be in Sonoma soon. She did not want to be recognized by the townspeople while she was on her urgent mission. As she walked back to the campsite, Fitz was walking back holding some freshly caught ducks. *What a great guy. He thought to find food for us,* she thought to herself and happily smiled at Fitz.

"Top of the morning to you," Fitz said as he arrived at the newly stoked fire that Nicola readied to cook their meal. "I thought I would get us some food and let you sleep in."

She smiled, cleared the hair from the front of her face, and said, "Thank you. That was very thoughtful of you."

After breakfast and some small talk, the two soon-to-be heroes made their way to Sonoma. A few hours later, which would have been quicker if Fitz didn't stop to check out every sound he heard, they arrived at the city. They made their way to the castle, which was in the center of the city. Nicola's disguise worked. No one in the city recognized her. When the two travelers made it to the castle gate,

Nicola took off her wig. They walked through the gate and found her aunt and uncle.

"Nicola!" her aunt exclaimed.

"Hello, Aunt Suzan," Nicola replied with a huge smile on her face. She always loved seeing her aunt Suzan.

"Why do we have the honor of your visit today?" questioned Suzan. "I didn't know you were going to make a trip to see us."

"I have some urgent news that concerns Sonoma. Fitz and I"—Fitz waved his hand to say hello to Aunt Suzan—"have made the journey here to warn you and Uncle Abraham about an attack from Insidiaville. More specifically, from the attack will come from the city of Desert Springs."

"Why would they attack us? We are at peace with them," Suzan confusingly questioned.

"We, both Fitz and I, have uncovered separate plots against our great kingdom. My husband"—Nicola rolled her eyes—"has been planning this for many years. I am just a prop in his plan," she said sadly.

"I never trusted him," interrupted Uncle Abraham, walking up behind the three of them. "What did the king and queen say about this news?"

"They sent me here with the news about the upcoming attack. They believed that you would trust me with the news of the attack. I need to hurry back to Aurumton City so I can warn my parents about the second part of the plan, the part that was uncovered by Fitz."

"What is the second part?" asked Aunt Suzan.

Fitz then told them his story about what he overheard, how he was captured, and how he was flung into a horse. There were looks of grave concern of the faces of Suzan and Abraham, though they chuckled at the part about Fitz hitting the horse because he was not seriously injured.

"Do not worry about your father. He is very well protected. Stay here tonight, get some rest, and leave tomorrow morning. We will also have our cooks prepare a great feast tonight. Our spies will check out what is going on in Desert Springs. This is concerning, and we will be ready for anything," said Aunt Suzan. "I will show you to your rooms, so you can rest if you want."

"May I go to the library?" asked Nicola.

Her favorite memories of her childhood were the summer days she spent in Sonoma. She loved to go to the library, the largest in the country. Her favorite book was called *The Legend of the Kingsbridge Lake Monster*. The book glowed red in color, contained stories of knights, a princess, magic, and a monster in the lake. On the way to her room, she made the stop by the library to pick up that book. When she got to her room, she laid down on the bed and started reading. Fitz, who had never picked up a book in his life, just smiled and went with Suzan to his room. Suzan had a doctor waiting in Fitz's room to look over his shoulder. After a treatment of a mixture of wintergreen, lavender, and peppermint oils, the pain subsided, and Fitz dozed off.

Nicola and Fitz rested a few hours. Fitz was awoken, and Nicola was pulled away from her book just as she finished reading it. The last page read…

> *The island will become corrupt*
> *after the passing of the three.*
> *The people will kill.*
> *Four generations will pass.*
> *A girl will be born,*
> *one with hair of gold*
> *and eyes of the sky;*
> *will find the magic*
> *and restore the island.*

Suzan told them that the feast was ready to eat. Quail, duck, trout, and a variety of vegetables were spread upon the table.

"You two need to eat up to regain your strength for tomorrow's journey," Aunt Suzan ordered.

"Fitz, please tell us about yourself?" inquired Uncle Abraham, wanting to make the atmosphere in the room less tense.

"I am a journeyman. I do what I can find for work. I have no real skills, just a few things here and there," answered Fitz.

"Do I know your parents? You look familiar. Where are you from?" questioned Uncle Abraham.

"I am from Silvager, the city of Tilton, more specifically. My parents worked for the king until they passed away when I was a boy." The conversation was interrupted by a large burp from Nicola, a glare by Aunt Suzan, and Fitz continued, "After that, I hung around the castle, learning anything I could from anyone who would teach me. After a few years, I left and have been on my own, just doing whatever I can find. Nothing special, I just live a simpleton's life."

"We do thank you for taking care of Nicola the last couple of days," said Suzan, smiling at Fitz.

Fitz responded, "It was not a problem. It has been an honor to help. Like everyone else in each kingdom, I do not want to have Caelon in power."

After dinner and small chitchat, the two went back to their rooms and went to sleep for the night. They both knew they needed rest to make the trip back to Aurumton City the next day.

The next morning came quickly.

After a hurried breakfast, Aunt Suzan gave Nicola a hug and said, "No matter what happens, remember you will be the queen someday of two kingdoms. You and Caelon are married, and there is no other heir to their throne. By marriage, you are the queen, and if something happens to Caelon, you are the one that will be the ruler. Only you can bring peace and unification to the two kingdoms. Take the route through the mountains. It is a hidden path that has not been traveled in hundreds of years. You will be safe, and the journey will be quicker." With those words, the travelers left on their return journey.

After the two of them left, Abraham's spies arrived back with their report about the activity in Desert Springs.

The chief scout announced, "There is no army activity going on in the area of Desert Springs. It looks like a setup to get Nicola separated from the safety of the Aurumton City palace."

"That is what I thought," replied Suzan. "I can only pray that she will be safe on her journey back."

CHAPTER 32

The Plan Starts

Prince Caelon paced around his bed chambers in his castle, waiting impatiently for his guards to return from their quest of the execution of Nicola. He looked out the window and into the distance.

"How can they take so long to get back?" he murmured to himself. "They only had one thing to do, kill a defenseless and pathetic little girl."

A few more long moments passed, and then the captain of the guard sprinted into Caelon's room.

"We cannot find her. We shot the prisoner at her, and somehow she managed to escape," said the captain of the guards.

"You shot the prisoner at her? Why would you so such a thing?" questioned Caelon with a fire building in his eyes.

"We had no stones for the catapult. We decided that the prisoner was expendable and that he would probably die when he collided with her," answered the guard captain, trying to sound smart as his actions.

"How did she get away?" Caelon demanded in a tone that made the walls tremble with fear.

"It took some time to get to the path because the forest is thick and overgrown. When we got to the path, all that was left was her broken horse and an empty potato sack," the captain of the guard answered with fear choking his voice.

"I gave you one command, to kill the princess, and you failed me. To make it worse, you *gave* her the only person that knows *my* plan, which means that she now knows my plan," Caelon roared.

The captain answered, "We failed you, and we failed our kingdom."

"Maybe this can work in our favor. While she is with her aunt and uncle, we can accelerate the plans. I have some poison that I could have the royal cook add to my parent's food tonight. By morning, they will be dead. That would give me complete control of Insidiaville. Then I will head to Aurumton City to leave a giant surprise for my wife, her parents dead. Then the only thing left would be to get rid of her and then both kingdoms will be mine," Caelon plotted out loud. "Then Tero will have to bow to my wishes because I will control the majority of the island."

The captain of the guard interrupted, "What do you want us to do?"

"Next time, follow your orders and keep an eye out for the escaped prisoner. We never had a chance to question him to find out who he is or what he knows. Right now, he is an enemy of Insidiaville. He is wanted dead or alive. You also have to make sure that my parents enjoy their last meal together," Caelon said as he rubbed his hands together.

"We serve your commands," the guard answered and bowed, thankful for his life.

After the guards left, Caelon quickly made his way to the kitchen to meet secretly with the cook.

"Elek, my old friend, I need you to add this spice to my parent's meal tonight. It is something that they have been asking for."

"What is it?" Elek, the cook, inquired.

Elek was an average man in build, standing at an average height with an average weight, short brown hair and brown eyes. He was a couple years older than Caelon and was not educated at all. He knew enough to speak properly because he cooked for the king and queen for many years. He had a kind of round stomach, and he also wheezed slightly when he breathed. Both of these could be attributed to the years of baking. He really had no skills in life, except he could cook. He dressed in what he could afford, which were plain brown clothes, which had many holes and patches. His face would often be dirty, but he did what he could to take care of his family. He could use any tool in the kitchen but had never touched a weapon for battle.

"You do not want to know, and please do not eat any of it. This is going to be a surprise for the king and queen, and don't tell anyone else," Caelon secretly commanded while handing the bottle to Elek.

Elek looked at the bottle and replied with a scared look on his face, "You want me to murder them? I don't want to be part of this."

"Remember, when they are gone, *I am* the king. I begged my parents to give you this job, and you will obey what I command of you. Nothing will happen to you, I promise you that. You and your family will be taken care of." With this, Caelon left the vial of poison with the cook.

Time seemed to drag on that day for Caelon. He went to the forest just to waste some time. The wind picked up and blew through the trees making the pinecones sing.

Finally, the time came for the royal dinner, and the king and queen ate their meals of seasoned yams and roasted duck. They offered some the meal to Caelon, who politely declined their offer, claiming he was not hungry due to an upset stomach. He did sit with his parents, and the three talked about the future plans for the kingdom and how they could become a partner kingdom with Silvager. This would allow the shipping routes to reopen and generate a steady and much-needed income for the country. The king and queen also scolded Caelon about his treatment of Nicola.

"Caelon, you need to be a better husband," was said by the queen.

"It would be better for the kingdom and for you in the long term," added the king.

After their conversation, the king and queen went to their chambers and fell asleep, never to wake up.

It was a long night for Caelon. The wind continued to howl through the castle walls all night, which added to his restlessness—

The plan is starting—he excitedly thought to himself, keeping him more awake.

Finally, the next morning arrived, and the news broke that the king and queen died in their sleep. Caelon went to their room to check to see if the news, which he already knew, was true. When he opened the door and he saw the king and queen lying lifeless, his heart smiled, but he started to cry on the outside—*My plan is working*—he thought to himself while the palace workers comforted him.

He said to the guards, "This morning I saw the cook in the kitchen holding a suspicious-looking bottle in his hand. Do you think he would poison my parent's food? I wasn't feeling well last, so I didn't eat. Instead, I sat with my parents while they ate. They seemed to be in fine spirit when they went to bed last night."

The guards hastily made their way to the kitchen and found an empty vial in the trash. The vial was labeled, "Hemlock Mandrake Poison," a poison known to leave no survivors.

"The cook poisoned the king and queen. Find him!" the commander of the royal guard commanded in a booming voice.

The guards, followed by a smiling Caelon, stormed the cook's house, where they found him feeding his flock of chickens.

"You are under arrest for the murder of the king and queen," the commander said with a stern look on his face.

"What?" the cook said in surprise. Then he said, "I was set up. Caelon made me add the poison to their food."

The commander interrupted, "You admit that you poisoned the king and queen."

"I did it under Caelon's orders," defended Elek.

"Why would I want to kill my parents? He is lying. Arrest him and kill *his* wife. Take the child and give him to the kingdom of Silvager as a slave. Tero should love the gift of young labor," ordered Caelon as he up walked behind the guards at the same time they were arresting the cook. "Kill her now so he can see what happens to people who murder the king and queen, then throw him in the dungeon."

With that order, the commander of the royal guard pulled out his sword and cut off the head of the cook's wife. Another guard tied the young boy's arms behind his back and carried him off while he was kicking and screaming.

The cook closed his eyes as the sword was drawn. He was mad at himself for not trusting in his own judgment the night before. Caelon lied to him, and it cost him everything. His family was gone. He was to be sentenced to death and would probably die before sundown. He never thought his life would turn out this way. All he wanted to do was to protect his family, but there was nothing he could do.

Caelon made his way back to *his* castle, smiling and almost skipping all the way, and got ready to make his way to Aurumton City to finish his plans. The commander of the guards gave Elek to another guard to haul off to the dungeon while he stayed to oversee the cleanup of the mess. However, Elek noticed that his hands were not tied tightly and that he had managed to loosen the knots even more by the time they reached the dungeon. When the guard went to open the large and heavy dungeon door, Elek freed his hands and punched the guard in the back of the head. The guard fell forward and hit his head on the door. The guard tried to turn around, but fell to the ground, knocked unconscious. Elek ran, faster than he ever had run in his life, toward the road to Aurumton City. He needed to see the only person that the country could trust, Princess Nicola.

CHAPTER 33

Kingsbridge Lake

Fitz and Nicola argued about which way to go. Nicola wanted to take the path that Aunt Suzan said to take and Fitz wanted to stay on the main road. Nicola's choice would be shorter, but it hadn't been traveled in a very long time. Fitz was sure the guards were gone, and the path would be safe. After ten minutes of arguing, Nicola pulled the "I'm the princess" and won the argument.

They started the journey toward the mountains, which really didn't take too long, and up into a mountain pass. Fitz noticed gold lying on the path. Mixed in the gold was a different color of dirt that had the color of ash. They cleared the path and noticed a lake in the distance. Nicola had seen many maps of the island but never remembered seeing a lake in the mountains. All she knew was mountains with no path through them.

As they approached the lake, the landscape changed. The mountains seemed to drop straight toward the lake. The lake was a midnight-blue color, some of the most beautiful water that Nicola and Fitz had ever seen. They stopped for a minute to admire the beauty of it all. It looked better than the famous magical water from Desert Springs. The sky reflected perfectly off the water, showing the fluffy clouds hanging in the sky. As they got close, they could hear the gentle ripples of waves that made a soft sound as they rolled into the sandy shore. To Nicola's surprise, there was a tower at the north end of the lake, and it looked just like the picture in the book.

"Did the lake monsters really exist?" she asked Fitz.

Fitz cautiously answered, "I don't know, but keep an eye out. This place is starting to scare me. Did you see the grave in the trees?"

The south side of the lake was covered in armor and a countless number of used arrows. It looked like an old battleground. Nicola was wondering if the book was about a real piece of history instead of a made-up fairy tale. If the book was true, then the spirit of the princess would still be in the tower. The spirit was allowed to help one person, the one that was worthy. In the book, no one was found worthy of the help. Nicola wondered if she would be worthy of the help from the spirit. Fitz wanted nothing to do with the tower, but just like last time, Nicola won the standoff.

As they approached the tower, Fitz stated, "I am waiting outside. There is nothing inside, and I do *not* want to waste my time looking around. I will go find some wood to make a campfire and get ready to spend the night here since we are about halfway home."

"Sounds good to me. I can't wait to see what is inside the tower. Maybe the spirit of the princess will help us with our journey," Nicola replied.

"Go look if you want. You need to grow up and not worry about fairy tales and old battles. We have a *real* fight that is about to happen," Fitz said with a little harshness in his voice.

Nicola looked at the door to the tower, and her mind flashed to when she was a baby lying in her crib. An image of a tower appeared above the baby. The tower slowly transformed into a lady with long, dark hair. The lady looked at Nicola and softly stroked her hair and said, "I will watch over and protect you. You *will* become a great queen and lead this island back to its former glory. Be strong and trust your heart." The lady slowly vanished into nothing. The vision left, and Nicola, not knowing what the vision meant, slowly made her way to the tower entrance.

Nicola entered the main door of the tower and slowly made her way up the winding stairway. At the halfway point of the stairs, there was a window that looked toward the lake. As Nicola looked out the window, she thought she saw a large creature in the middle of the lake dive under the water. *Is the book really true?* she continued to wonder. When she arrived at the top of the stairs, there was a locked door. Nicola knocked on the door three times, but nothing happened. The lock looked old and rusted. She tried to break it off, but she was not strong enough to break the lock. With her hope dashed, she started to make her way down when she heard a click. She turned around and saw the lock was opened.

Nicola slowly opened the door and walked in. There she found an old bed and some old clothes lying around. It looks like no one had lived here for a very long time. In the middle of the room was a midnight-blue mist, in the shape of a cloud.

As she approached the mist, she heard a pleasant but a thunderous voice, "Who dares to enter my chambers?"

Nicola lowered her head and said, "I am Nicola, Princess of Aurumton and Insidiaville."

"Why are you here?" the voice continued.

"I, I, I, I," Nicola was a little frightened as she spoke to the cloud, "I read a book long ago, and everything in the book is here. I even saw the lake monster. I was hoping that the spirit in the tower could help me on my journey back to Aurumton City."

"You saw the lake monster? You were not frightened?" the voice prodded with questions.

Nicola quickly answered, "I saw the monster. At first, I was scared, but the monster was in the middle of the lake, and I was in the tower."

The voice paused for a brief moment before saying, "Why did you make a journey to the tower?"

"I wanted to know if my heart was worthy to be the one. I need help with my journey," said Nicola sadly.

"I am the spirit, and I find your heart true and pure. I have been watching over you since the time of your birth, you, the child with hair of gold and eyes of the sky. You have been destined to bring unity back to the island. What help do you need on your journey?" the voice echoed.

Nicola, talking quickly, said, "Caelon, the prince of Insidiaville, is planning to kill my parents and take over Aurumton. I am on my way back to inform my parents and stop Caelon from taking over."

"I cannot help with your parents. Their fate is something that I cannot interfere with, but your fate is what I am destined to help with. I will join you in your quest, and I will give you help where I can." After the spirit said that, the cloud slowly transformed into a woman. "My name is Karisma. I am here to help you. My destiny has long been to guide you and help you in bringing unity back to the island."

Nicola looked confused at the sight of a woman coming out of the blue mist.

"What do you mean?" she asked.

Karisma answered, "Long ago, when the island was formed by the wizard, a destiny was set forth. Many knights came here on a quest to rescue a beautiful and magical princess. After that, the wizard hid the island and made people forget about the quests. Years later, a prince found the island. The prince became corrupted by his own desires and killed the wizard. Some years later, three brothers found the island and became the first kings of the island. Their sons corrupted the island into what it has turned into today. The corruption dissolved the peace and unity, and the island's magic was extinguished. Your destiny is to restore the peace and unity back to the island."

"Are you the princess that was locked in the tower all those years?" Nicola asked, hoping to learn more.

Karisma smiled and answered, "Yes, I am the princess. The magic will not allow me to age. The magic gives me powers and you coming here to this tower has brought the magic back to me and to the whole island."

"All those times that I read the book, I never knew it was a real story." Nicola smiled, thinking about her book.

Karisma answered, "The book was written to teach the history of the island, but it has been long forgotten."

"I am extremely humbled and honored," Nicola said to Karisma. "My friend is gathering some wood for a fire. We are planning to camp here tonight and continue the journey tomorrow. Would you join us tonight? I am sure that Fitz will have something for us to eat."

Karisma smiled at Nicola and replied, "Let's go. I haven't walked down the stairs in years."

They laughed, and the two ladies made their way down the spiral stairs to the campfire, where Fitz was cooking some freshly caught lake trout.

"Hello," he said cautiously as he saw the two ladies walking toward him. "I take it you found someone in the tower."

"Good guess, Fitz," Nicola sarcastically said. "This is Karisma. She is going to be joining us for the rest of our journey."

"Nice to meet you, Karisma," said Fitz, looking a bit confused at having two companions now.

"Hello, Fitz," replied Karisma. "Thank you for cooking some fish and making a warm fire. It has been a long time since I have seen one of these."

The three talked over dinner and watched the fiery orange sunset, which gave way to a black, star-filled sky. Nicola and Fitz drifted off to sleep, and Karisma watched the moon's reflection on the lake. She thought of all that had happened since Ulric created the island, trusting that this was the girl of the prophecy.

The next morning, Nicola and Fitz awoke to the smell of some more fish that Karisma caught for them. After a satisfying breakfast, the three set off to complete the journey to Aurumton City. Karisma snapped her fingers, and two horses appeared. Karisma rode with Nicola on one horse, and Fitz rode the other. He also insisted that he would lead the group down the remains of the old path. The path was overgrown with trees and shrubs, so travel was extremely slow, but eventually, the three made it to the south entrance of the city.

CHAPTER 34

Meeting at the Palace

Caelon arrived outside Aurumton City and found his army encamped on the north end of the city. He was informed that the army was still waiting on the delivery of weapons from Silvager, but Caelon did not care. His only goal now was to kill the king and queen of Aurumton then to find his wife and get rid of her.

Caelon wondered around the camp and eventually conferred with his general. He told him about the events of the previous day. Now that he was king, the army will have to obey his commands. The general, not wanting to cause trouble, wanted to know why he would attack Nicola, the new queen of Insidiaville, and murder her parents. The queen had the same powers as the king. Caelon lifted his sword to the chest of the general, and he agreed to obey Caelon's commands. He got the army ready to attack on command. They only thing they needed was the weapons, which Tero and Silvager should be delivering soon.

Elek, the cook who had earlier been arrested for the murder of the king and queen of Insidiaville, arrived a few minutes behind Caelon's arrival. He thought the south entrance would be his best chance to avoid being seen and captured again by Caelon. He only hoped that Nicola was at the castle so he could warn her about what was going to happen, and maybe he hoped that she could help him.

Elek slowly made his way around the outskirts of the city without being seen. Just as he made it to the south entrance, Nicola and her friends walked up from the hidden path.

"Nicola!" he yelled with some excitement in his voice.

Fitz pulled out his sword, pointed it at Elek, and stated, "I know you. You are from Insidiaville. Better yet, you are from Facultas, and you work for Caelon personally."

"Not anymore," replied Elek. "Caelon framed me for the murder of the king and queen. He had my wife killed in front of me, and my child was taken away and given to Tero as a slave. I escaped the guard and made my way here to see Nicola. I can only hope that she can help me. I also can tell you that Caelon is on the north side of the city with his army!"

"That is a lot quicker than the four weeks you told me about, Fitz," Nicola fearfully said. "You did not say anything about the murder of his parents."

"I did not hear anything about that. I told you everything that I overheard," Fitz reassured her.

While the four talked, Caelon's army received the weapons from Silvager. The army moved from the camp to the north side gate and waited for Caelon's command. Caelon entered the castle and found the king and queen in the upper throne room in the center of the castle.

"Are you surprised to see me? Bow down before me, the king of Insidiaville, and I might let you live. You, guards, close and lock the doors! Where is my wife? I want her to see this," Caelon boastfully commanded

"The king of Insidiaville?" the king of Aurumton replied in a shocked voice.

Caelon laughed and happily said, "My parents are dead. I am the king now, and soon I will be king here. My army waits outside. Look for yourself. I will finish what my grandfather started before you murdered him."

"You are mad. He attacked us, much like you want to do today. I was a young boy trying to save my family. You need help. Your grandfather was overcome with greed and lust for power, and you are becoming the same. You married my daughter in the name of peace between our countries," the king reprimanded.

Caelon, not wanting to listen to anything, yelled back, "You fell for my plan. I needed to use her to get to this. Don't worry about her. I will take care of her 'until death does us part.' She will be joining you soon, I will make sure of that. Her beauty sickens me, and it will finally rot away when she is dead."

Nicola and her friends made their way inside the castle, to the fork in the hallway. One way led to the throne room, the other to the bedchambers.

Nicola said, "We need to split up and find my parents fast. Fitz, you come with me. Karisma, you and…what is your name?"

"Elek. Elek, the former cook of Insidiaville," he replied with a smile.

Nicola commanded, "Karisma and Elek, you go together and head down the hall toward the bedchambers. Fitz and I will head to the throne room."

Karisma reminded Nicola, "Remember, I cannot interfere with the fate of your parents, but I can help you."

The two groups split and hurried to their destinations in the castle. Karisma and Elek arrived at the bedchambers first.

"Your Majesties? Are you there?" yelled Elek.

There was no answer, just the howl of the wind through the windows. Karisma looked around the room with no signs that anyone was in the area. The two of them turned back to find Nicola and Fitz in the throne room.

Nicola and Fitz arrived at the throne room, shortly after Karisma and Elek arrived at the bedchamber, to find the doors have been shut and locked.

"Mom? Dad?" she screamed with terror in her voice.

All she heard back were screams, screams that sounded like someone was being stabbed. Fitz, in an instant, decided to kick the door open. Nicola ran inside the throne room as fast as the door opened. She opened her eyes as she entered and saw Caelon holding his sword, dripping with blood, and both her parents lying on the floor.

He smiled at her and teased, "Nicola, welcome to the party. I was wondering when my wife would join me. I left a gift on the floor for you to open."

Nicola yelled at the top of her lungs, "You will pay for your crimes against the throne of Aurumton."

"And who is going to stop me? You, my lovely beautiful wife, will soon be joining them." With this, Caelon walked to the window and shot a flare to signal his army to attack the expecting city.

The general saw the flare and ordered his troops to attack.

Just then, the captain of the guard said, "Sir, we do not have any ammunition."

"What do you mean there's no ammunition?" the general asked.

The captain, who had to inform Caelon a few days earlier about not having stones for the catapult, sadly said, "We opened the crates and found the weapons, but there was no ammunition."

The general said, "We have been tricked."

As he said this, a loud volley of muskets was heard. The general and half the army fell dead. A second volley sounded and more of the army fell. A third volley sounded, and the rest of Caelon's army was gone. The whole army was wiped out in less than a few minutes.

Back in the throne room, Caelon bragged, "Do you hear that sound my wife? That is the sound of my victory. This city will be mine in a few minutes. My army has been waiting for this attack all day, and they will not take any prisoners. I think a victory kiss is in order for the new king before I kill you."

The back door to the throne room exploded, and the whole room shook. Caelon, a bit startled, turned around and saw Tero walking into the throne room. Fitz grabbed Nicola by her hair and tied her hands behind her back.

"Hello, brother," said Fitz to Tero.

"Brother?" questioned Nicola with great fear. "You have been lying this whole time?"

Fitz tightly placed his hand over Nicola's mouth and answered, "Of course. I followed my brother to get information from Caelon. I knew he wouldn't recognize me since my parents never let me out of the castle. Before I followed Caelon, I took the stones out of the catapult's carriage. The whole thing was a setup. You never noticed that we were being followed the whole time. I talked to Tero's personal guards the whole journey. You never saw them following us. They gave the information to Tero. He knew when we would arrive here. It was an easy capture. My brother wanted a treasure that would show the whole island the power of Silvager. That treasure is you, Nicola, and you are now ours."

"Thank you, Fitz, my brother, you secured my beautiful treasure." Tero looked at Caelon and said, "I told you 50 percent. Instead, you insulted me with a weak offer. I never wanted to take over the island, but you opened an opportunity for me. All I wanted was your wife. She controls the island. Thank you for making this easy by killing your parents and also killing the king and queen of Aurumton. I should let you live and suffer in the prison, but"—Tero grabbed his sword, and with one swift move, he cut off Caelon's head—"murder is punishable by death. Now, my treasure, what to do with you? You know too much. You will not bow down to my wishes. You still have too much power with the people. I could kill you and frame Caelon, but that would be too easy. I'd rather make you my personal slave. You will live in the castle, never to see the light outside, and do all of my commands. Someday the people will forget all about you."

Just then, a dragon flew in and grabbed Nicola. It used its giant tail to fling Fitz across the room. Fitz crashed out the window. He died when he hit the ground. Nicola, scared beyond belief, looked at the dragon and saw its midnight-blue eyes.

"Karisma?" she whispered.

The dragon winked then grabbed Elek and flew out of the castle.

CHAPTER 35

In the Ruins

Tero looked with great surprise as the dragon grabbed his treasure and flew off. There had not been a dragon sighting for many years on the island. The dragon was flying too high to have his army shoot. *Next time I will be prepared,* he thought to himself.

Tero looked through the window toward his brother and said, "Revenge will honor your death, my brother. Your sacrifice will not be in vain. Nicola will pay for this. She will bow down to Silvager."

Tero's army commanders made their way to the throne room. They gave the news that Tero already knew about Fitzpatrick's death.

Tero looked at the commanders and gave the murderous order, "Burn the castle. Take no palace prisoners. If the people want to join me, so be it. If they resist, then kill them."

Tero walked out of the castle as the red flames rose behind him. As the castle burned, Tero made his way through the city toward his army's camp, not stopping until he reached his tent. There he met with the army's generals.

"We need to find Nicola. We need to slay the dragon in order to rid the island of this treacherous pest. Nicola must die," Tero said with a stern look.

With that, he stormed out of his tent, mounted his horse, and stormed in the direction of Tilton, the capital of Silvager. The generals stayed behind to finish the business left by Tero.

Nicola and her friends flew to the south and landed in some ruins. The ruins looked like an old castle, one that had not seen people in hundreds of years.

"What is this place?" asked Nicola. "I do not remember hearing about ruins on the island."

Karisma transformed back to her human form and answered, "This is the lost city of Unidade. The three brothers that became the first kings of the island made their castle here. The ruins were hidden as well as taken out of every history book. The tombs of the three kings are here. This is a place of great magic, plus we can stay hidden for a while."

Nicola humbly said to Karisma, "Thank you for saving me from Tero and from Fitz. He really tricked me. I had no idea that he was Tero's brother or that he was using me for their own gain."

"I did not trust him from the start, but I can see people's true heart. I am also not allowed to interfere with anyone's destiny, but like I told you before, I can help with yours," Karisma answered.

"Thank you for also saving me," Elek added.

"Your heart is true and pure," Karisma smiled at Elek. "Caelon has killed enough. The island may never recover from his actions. Tero may have served justice, but it is only temporary. He will not stop at taking over now that the power has shifted to him. We need to stop him. He has become angry about his brother's death, and that anger will lead to a lust for power, a lust not seen before."

Elek asked, "What do we need to do? Nicola and I have lost a lot. No one else needs to lose what they love for the name of power and control. What can I do to help stop this?"

Nicola and her friends set up a shelter next to the ruins. Elek caught a rabbit and cooked it for a meal. Karisma suggested that they remain here for a few weeks so they could rest and devise a plan to stop Tero. The plan was to rally the others in Aurumton and Insidiaville to aid in stopping Tero and his powerful army. After talking for a couple of hours, they finalized a plan. Elek and Karisma would travel city to city with an urgent message from Queen Nicola. Nicola, with lots of protest, was to stay at the ruins of Unidade on one condition—that she could make one trip to Sonoma to pick up supplies that the three would need to survive at the ruins. After the trip, Nicola would be hidden to avoid being found by Tero and his scouts. As long as she remained under the magic of Unidade, she would be safe.

The sun started to set, and the three of them watched the glowing red ball fall behind the trees; the smoke and red glow from the burning castle could be seen in the distance. Nicola felt her heart sink as the smoke rose in the distant sky.

Nicola eventually fell asleep that night, but she kept thinking about the events of the past couple of days. She was scared; technically she was the queen of two kingdoms. Her parents were not around to help her anymore. She tossed and turned most of the night and heard a loud rumble. Nicola got up to have a look. She followed the sounds she heard to the tombs. It was night, but the moon shown so brightly she could see as if it were the day. She saw some rocks falling, but what caught her attention was a bright glowing golden cloud in the middle of the tomb. As she approached the cloud, she heard her father's voice, "Nicola, do not worry about your mother and I. We will always be with you. Also, do not worry about being the queen. Long ago, you were promised to bring peace and unity back to the whole island. It is a prophecy that we have long known but never told you. Karisma will lead you to stop Tero."

"What do you mean, long ago?" Nicola asked with the golden cloud glowing in her eyes.

"The three brothers buried in this tomb were the first three kings of the island. They ruled separate kingdoms but always kept unity and peace for the people on the island. When their offspring grew, they became corrupted by greed, envy, and lust, and the island lost its unity. After the unity failed, the peace stopped. As the peace stopped, the magic of the island faded from existence. Before the magic stopped completely, you were to be born with the ability to bring the unity and peace back. When you made your way to Kingsbridge Lake, the magic started to come back. As the peace comes back, the magic will become stronger. With this, the island will become one again," her father answered as his voice echoed in the tomb.

Nicola asked with the tone of a child, "How do I stop Tero? He is very powerful."

"Learn the magic while you are in the ruins…" As Nicola's father said this, the golden cloud moved and covered Nicola, and with a flash, the cloud entered her body.

"Did you find anything in here?" asked Karisma, who quietly followed Nicola into the tomb.

"Yes, that was a lot of information I just learned," Nicola said with glowing excitement on her face.

Karisma smiled and answered, "I am sure you have lots of questions. We will have time for that later. It is time to head to Sonoma."

"Let's go!" exclaimed Nicola.

Karisma transformed into the dragon, and Nicola climbed on her back. Elek, who was soundly sleeping curled in a ball, was suddenly awakened by being scooped in the dragon's talons. He screamed with a high-pitch, almost girly sound.

"Hey, could you keep the screaming down," Nicola playfully scolded. "We don't want to wake anyone up."

"You have a better seat riding on the dragon than I do. I was scooped up in the long, sharp talons," remarked Elek.

"I didn't scratch you. I was gentle on the pickup," replied Karisma.

The three made their way to Sonoma in about five minutes, which was a lot quicker on a dragon than on a horse.

CHAPTER 36

Becoming a Queen

Karisma, the dragon, landed a half mile from the entrance to the city of Sonoma. There she transformed into a horse, a black thoroughbred, sleek and strong, with midnight-blue eyes, one that was worthy of a queen to ride. Nicola mounted the horse. Elek, with some slight complaining, walked along the side. Karisma assured him that he could ride on the dragon on the way back to the ruins.

After a brief discussion, the three made their way the last mile into the city. They walked through the city without stopping. The people of Sonoma watched Nicola, with great surprise that she was alive, as she approached the castle. Nicola jumped off Karisma and led her into the main gate of the castle. There Karisma changed back into her human form.

"Good to see you again," said Elek.

"Thank you. It is good to be back in this form," replied Karisma while stretching her back.

"Hey, you two, we have a task to complete here. We need to focus on that task," Nicola said. "We need to find Aunt Suzan and Uncle Abraham."

"Now you are starting to sound like a queen," Karisma happily stated.

Nicola smiled as the three made their way through the castle, finding Suzan and Abraham in the courtyard.

"Nicola! We were so worried when we saw the smoke last night. We sent some scouts to inform us of what had happened. They should be returning sometime tonight."

"Tero burned the castle," Nicola sadly said with tears in her eyes.

"Tero did what? What happened?" questioned Uncle Abraham.

"In a short story, we arrived, Fitz, Karisma, and I. Caelon had the throne room locked. Fitz busted the door down, and my parents were already dead, killed by Caelon. While he was in the process of capturing me, Tero blew the other door down and made his way to Caelon with the news of a trick. When this happened, Fitzpatrick grabbed me and tied me up, informed me that he was Tero's brother and had been using me the whole time. Tero then killed Caelon. After that happened, Karisma and Elek saved me from Tero. During the rescue, Fitz was killed. After we escaped the castle, Tero burned it." Nicola took a deep breath to gather her wind back after saying that fast.

She tried to hold back tears in her eyes, but that did not last long.

"Wow, so much has happened. I am sorry about your parents. Thanks to you, Karisma and Elek, for saving Nicola," said Aunt Suzan. "Why did you come here? You know that Tero will come here to look for you."

Nicola hugged Aunt Suzan and said, "We need to gather some supplies so we can get our plan ready. Karisma and Elek are going from town to town to rally support for the fight against Tero. I am going to be in hiding."

Abraham asked, "Where are you hiding?"

Karisma interrupted, "We cannot tell anyone that. With Tero's power, we don't want to take any chances."

"Understood," said Abraham.

"What do you need from us?" asked Aunt Suzan.

"Food!" Elek said with excitement, which made Nicola and Karisma laugh.

"Blankets would be nice also. I also need some paper, ink, and sealing wax so I can write the official letters to the people in the other cities," Nicola added while thinking. "There is plenty of wood for fires. We have a shelter to keep us from the elements. Just those few items are all we will need."

"Take what you need. Also remember, you are always welcome here," answered Suzan.

"Thank you. We will load up quickly," said Nicola.

The five of them loaded crates of food and blankets. After the crates were loaded, Nicola said her goodbyes. Karisma transformed back into the dragon. Nicola and Elek, just as Karisma promised, climbed on her back. She scooped up the crates in the talons and took off, this time high into the sky, trying not to be seen. Nicola loved the sudden ascent into the sky while poor Elek just screamed into Nicola's ears.

The view from high up was incredible. Nicola could see the whole island. She could also still see the smoking remains of her parent's palace.

"Where are the ruins located?" she asked Karisma.

"They are in the center of the island. Hold on tight." As Karisma said this, she dove straight down to the ruins.

Again, Elek screamed at the top of his lungs. The sudden descent turned into the gentlest landing.

Elek jumped off quickly and then ran behind a tree to throw up. The girls laughed at Elek's misfortune. "It's not funny," was heard from behind the tree.

After Elek rested a bit, he helped in unpacking the crates. When this task was done, he and Karisma went off to gather wood for the fires; Nicola went inside the tombs to start her letters. There she sensed the magic of the island.

As Karisma and Elek walked through the woods, Karisma said, "You have a destiny to fulfill also. I will help you in doing so."

"What do you mean? I have lost everything, thanks to Caelon's tricks. I have no home. I lost my wife, and my only child was taken to Tero's slave camps. I do not have a way to make an income. I have nothing," questioned Elek

"You can gain something," Karisma replied, looking at the tombs where Nicola was busy writing.

"No. You don't mean...," Elek cautiously answered.

Karisma wisely answered, "Your destiny lies in helping Nicola unify the island. You will find love again. Everything you lost, and more, will be given back to you."

"I am a cook who has no other skills. She is a queen. She rides a dragon with bravery. I scream and get sick," Elek answered in disbelief.

Karisma smiled and said, "True, but Nicola sees your heart. One of her gifts is the ability to look past faults and see the good in everyone. That is why Fitzpatrick was able to trick her so easily. She saw the good in him as he helped her. I knew right away, by the way he was looking around that he was up to something. You have a good and caring heart, one that will be full of love when the battle is over. Until then, you have a lot of work to do. First, I will teach you how to use a sword."

"Really? You, a person that is full of magic, can teach me to fight? What would you know about fighting?" Elek smartly asked.

Elek sarcastically smiled, and Karisma grabbed a large stick and smacked him on the back of the head.

"What? Didn't you see that coming?" Karisma said while laughing.

The rest of the day was spent with Karisma teaching Elek how to swordfight. The sounds of sticks hitting each other echoed through the trees. Elek was a fast learner. He had finished with only a few bumps and bruises. "Battle scars," he proudly boasted.

As the sun started to set, the two made their way back to ruins to set up camp for the night. As the fire started to roar, Nicola walked out of the tombs. She had a bright golden glow around her.

She said, "I have finished the first letter." She walked over to the fire and sat down next to Elek. "Thank you for all of your help," she said to Elek.

Then she gave him a big hug. Elek smiled and looked at Karisma with some disbelief in his heart.

The following week was spent pretty much the same. Nicola would enter the ruins, write letters, and come out covered in a glow-ing golden color that would surround her. Karisma continued to teach Elek how to fight. After a week, Elek became an elite swordsman. She also helped him overcome his screaming fits while riding a dragon.

After the week was up, it was decided that the time had come for Karisma and Elek to deliver the letters to the people of the island. Nicola hoped that the people would overcome their fear and follow her.

CHAPTER 37

Tero's Anger

Back in Tilton, Tero met with his army generals to devise a plan to stop the dragon and recapture Nicola, this time to kill her. It was decided that they needed better guns, ones that would shoot higher and farther to stop the dragon. The guns also needed to be more powerful, since dragons were known to have thick skin. The army started to work on these new guns immediately. He wanted a final battle in at the ruins of Aurumton City. Tero's spies returned to him and reported that the people in Sonoma helped Nicola and her friends by giving them supplies. Tero responded to the news by having the city destroyed.

After the meeting, Tero left to go back to Aurumton City. Upon his arrival, he met with the army commanders he had left to guard the ruins of the city. Tero gave them the news of the upcoming final battle. Tero also informed the commanders of the new secret weapon, one that would defeat the dragon. To add insult to Nicola, Tero flew his kingdom's flag in the middle of the burned palace. The flag struck fear in every sailor who had seen it up close. The flag was a black flag with a white skull that was crossed behind with blood-red muskets.

After Tero raised the flag, he hastily made his way to the gold mines that were close to the city. His army was still raiding the mines, obtaining gold and wealth for Silvager. Seeing all the carts of gold heading toward Silvager made Tero smile. He had everything, except the final victory when he would defeat Nicola. Then he would rule the island.

Tero left the mines, and he went back to the field where his army was encamped. There he took his generals to survey the upcoming battlefield. Tero wanted to know everything about the field: where the holes were, where the grass was taller, where the slight inclines started and ended. A soldier could trip in a hole. Taller grass made the troops slower. The slight inclines could speed up the soldiers or slow them down. Little details like this could be the difference between victory and or defeat. Tero was determined not to lose to Nicola. The more he thought about the battle, the more his hatred grew toward Nicola and the more he wanted her dead.

That night Tero camped with the army. The army talked about the upcoming battle. The army was excited about a battle since most of them had never been in one. They had trained long and hard for this, but now the time was upon them to show they were true Silvagerian heroes. They also talked about Fitzpatrick. Hearing this talk made Tero's inner anger boil. How he wanted revenge on Nicola. He wanted it now, but none of the scouts could locate her.

The next day, still filled with a deep anger, Tero made his way back to Tilton. This time with his brother's remains. Tero believed that Fitzpatrick deserved a hero's burial. When he arrived, the burial preparations began. Tero also met with his generals to make the final plans for the defeat of Nicola.

CHAPTER 38

Rally the Island

Elek climbed up on Karisma and took off to make a trip back to Sonoma. As they got close, they could see smoke in the distance. Karisma's heart feared the worst. As they arrived at Sonoma, her heart sank when she found the city was gone.

They needed to get Nicola's message out, and fast, to have any chance of stopping Tero's powerful army. Elek suggested they head to Desert Springs, and Karisma agreed. They took off, leaving the ruins of Sonoma behind. They arrived a few minutes later, and they went to the town's center, and Karisma read Nicola's letter.

> *To my people, all inhabits of the island,*
> *As you have heard, there was an attack on Aurumton. The king and queen are dead, killed by Prince Caelon. During the attack, Caelon was beheaded by Tero. This leaves me, Nicola, as the queen of Aurumton and Insidiaville. Tero has his own plans for ruling the island. We all have a common enemy in Tero, the power-hungry pirate and king of Silvager. We need to join together to stop him from taking over the island.*
> *I ask, no, I beg that each one of you help in stopping Tero. In about one week's time, there was to*

be a celebration for my birthday party. I want that day to be the day that the island is liberated from Tero and his rule.

Please join me and my friends, Karisma and Elek, at the spot where the palace once stood in Aurumton City. Instead of a celebration, we will stop Tero.

Thank you for your help,
Queen Nicola
Together we will succeed!

After rallying the people of Desert Springs to Nicola's cause, Karisma and Elek slowly flew back to Nicola to give the good and bad news of the day. Nicola was happy that Desert Springs was on her side, but the guilt of getting supplies from Sonoma was tearing her up inside. She walked into the forest and cried most the night. Karisma and Elek tried to comfort her, but even in her discomfort, she politely declined their offers.

Each day through the next two weeks, Karisma and Elek traveled to a different city to deliver the queen's message. When Elek returned each day to the ruins, Nicola always gave him a hug.

The last trip was a trip home for Elek to Facultas. This brought up many memories for Elek. As Karisma flew near the city, Elek looked down as found his old house, and some tears came to of his eyes. Yet he had a job to do that would save the island from the evil Tero. Elek held his emotions inside and got ready to do his duty.

Karisma chose to land on the sandy beach just to the south of the port. It was empty due to the plundering pirates of Silvager. Elek hoped that the port could come back to life and that Insidiaville could regain its former glory of being a great farmland with a busy seaport. He hoped that Nicola could make that happen after the war was over with Tero. He knew deep down that if they won the battle then she would make his hope become a reality.

On the way to the town center, Elek told Karisma about the event that happened to the king and queen of Insidiaville. He told her the story of how Caelon framed him for the murder. He also told

Karisma how his wife was murdered in front of him by Caelon and how his child was taken away.

"The pain will end soon, Elek," Karisma told him and waved her hand over Elek's head.

Some blue mist fell on Elek's head, and as the mist covered him, his sadness faded away. All he thought about now was helping Nicola. He wanted to get back quickly to see her.

The two slowly made it to the town center, trying not to be seen, but a guard was heard yelling, "Arrest that man. He murdered the king and queen." Three guards came running, but Karisma used the blue mist to stop them.

The lead guard stopped in his tracks and said in a confused tone, "Why were we running? What are we doing? Why did we leave our post? Let's go back to standing guard."

At the town center, Elek bravely and confidently read Queen Nicola's letter to the towns-people with great authority. The towns-people were excited to hear that Nicola survived the attack. She was their queen, which was something the people had wished for long ago. The same guards who almost arrested Elek moments ago pledged their support to their new queen. They left to gather all the other guards, who in turn gathered what was left of Insidiaville's army.

As Elek and Karisma left, the army of Insidiaville could be seen starting their march to Aurumton City. Elek and Karisma smiled at this site. They made a fast flight to give the news to Nicola.

When they arrived, Elek was greeted with a kiss on the cheek from Nicola.

She whispered in his ear, "Thank you for all of your help."

Elek, blushing, replied with a nervous, squeaky voice, "You are most welcome, Your Majesty."

Nicola laughed at the sound of Elek's voice cracking.

Karisma reported the news of Insidiaville's army making their way to Aurumton City. Nicola had a big smile when she heard the news.

"It's time we get ready for battle," Nicola boldly said. "Tomorrow we will go to meet the people, our people, at the city. There we will put a stop to Tero!"

CHAPTER 39

Ready for Battle

The night before the impending battle, Nicola and her friends stayed at the ruins. Before they went to sleep for the night, Nicola brought the group inside the tomb, the place where she spent her days.

As the three approached the center of the triangularly shaped tomb, the main chamber where the three brothers were buried, the walls shook. After the shaking stopped, a golden mist appeared from the three sides of the room. Elek was too frightened to look. Karisma assured Elek that everything was going to be okay. As the mist came closer, it transformed into three human shapes.

As the mist continued to change into three large men, the three brothers, Nicola introduced Elek to the brothers, "This is Cass, the farmer. He was the first king of Insidiaville. This is Goran, the wealth keeper, and the first king of Aurumton. This is Salem, the peace-keeper, the first king of Silvager."

"Nice to meet you all," Elek's voice cracked.

Nicola smiled and said, "These three kings have taught me the history and magic of the island. When I first met Karisma, the magic, which was lost due to the corruption of the sons, was restored. The kings have also been helping in preparation for the battle."

"Tero needs to be stopped. His power-driven rage could end the island forever," boomed the voice of Salem.

"We agree," echoed the voices of Goran and Cass.

Some stone fell as the voices echoed in the tomb.

"They taught you magic?" questioned Elek, sounding confused.

Nicola slightly rolled her eyes and answered, "Yes, like the magic that Karisma uses. I can change into a misty cloud. This will be able to aid us greatly in the upcoming battle. I have not learned how to transform to different objects, but that will come as I learn more."

"What is the plan for the upcoming battle?" asked Elek, hoping the answer would be there would be no battle.

Goran thunderous voice answered, "You will need to use the forest surrounding the battlefield to hide your army from Tero's weapons. If they have clear shots, they will defeat you. You have Karisma's magic. You also have Nicola's magic. The magic used together will be impossible to stop, even for the advanced weapons."

"Be smart. Be brave. Be strong," Cass boasted.

"Nicola will lead the island to peace. The prophecy was foretold long ago by the wizard whose house stood at the sight of this tomb," Salem proclaimed.

"You must go now. Get your rest. Travel safe. Nicola, be strong," the three brothers said together as they faded back to a mist then disappeared.

"Wow!" exclaimed Elek. "I never knew."

"Hard to believe, isn't it?" replied Nicola while bumping her hip into Elek's.

The three made their way out of the tomb and back to their campsite for their final night.

"The magic of the tomb is what keeps this old city hidden. I hope to return this city to what it once was," said Nicola.

Karisma smiled at the sound of hearing that.

Elek started a fire and cooked a fine meal of deer with some wild onions. The three ate until they were full. Nicola moved to Elek to give him a goodnight kiss.

"I love you," she whispered into his ear.

Elek, with a giant smile, replied, "I love you too."

The sunset with a spectacular display of purples and reds. The three fell asleep as the full moon rose on the horizon. A lone wolf could be heard off in the distance.

Morning came quickly. Nicola awoke to the sound of the Blue Vangas as the sun rose. She wondered if they were the same ones she heard a few days ago. She grabbed a container of water and decided to dump it on Elek. As the cold water splashed on him, he screamed, waking Karisma up.

"What was that for?" Elek asked.

Nicola answered with glowing eyes and a half smirk, half smile. Karisma just shook her head.

Elek got up quickly after the shock of cold water and got ready for the trip to what was left of Aurumton City. Karisma went inside the tomb for a few moments. He prepared a quick meal for the three to eat before the battle, hoping deep down that it was not his last meal.

When Karisma came out of the tomb, she was illuminated with a glowing blue color.

"Now is the time," she said as she transformed into the dragon.

The two climbed on her back. With a quick movement of her wings, the three soared high above the island and made haste to the city.

As they arrived, Nicola looked down and saw the burned palace from above.

"Use this feeling of loss when you lead your people today," Karisma reminded her.

Nicola's eyes swelled with tears when she saw the Silvager flag in the ruins. As they descended to the palace, Karisma blew a fireball out her mouth that destroyed the Silvager flag that flew in the center of the once majestic palace.

As they landed, people came out from hiding to greet their queen.

The crowd of people yelled, "Long live Queen Nicola."

Karisma changed back into her human form, which amazed the crowd of people. Nicola waved her hand at the people and smiled.

Nicola made her way to the top of the palace ruins, next to the still smoldering flag, to address the crowd. She took a few deep breaths and closed her eyes.

She looked at Elek and loudly proclaimed, "A few weeks ago, my parents were slain here. Caelon paid for his crimes. Now, today is the day that Tero will be stopped. It will be a hard-fought battle that we can win if you trust me, your humble queen. With your help, the island will be *one*. Are you with me?"

The giant crowd of soldiers and townspeople, in unison, loudly chanted, "Long live Queen Nicola."

The men waved their swords, bows, and pitchforks in the air. Nicola smiled at the response and looked toward the sky and smiled.

"Karisma and Elek will give you your assignments. Victory will be ours!" cried Nicola.

CHAPTER 40

Battle in the Field

As everyone got their assignments, they made their way to the locations in the forest to be hidden from the mighty guns of Silvager. The soldiers were excited yet somewhat fearful. Nicola was concerned for the people, but she was ready to lead them. Elek took a place next to Nicola, in the southern end of the field near the eastern gate.

Elek looked at Nicola and said, "Happy birthday."

Nicola replied with a smile and small kiss on his cheek. Karisma took a spot just next to the gate behind Nicola and Elek.

The field was about two hundred yards long and about one hundred fifty yards wide. The grass in the field was about knee high and rather thick. The west end of the field was where the giant city gates once stood, the place where Caelon's army was slain three weeks earlier. The north end of the field, where the army of Silvager camped, was wooded with a road that led through the mountains and to the city of Tilton. The east end of the field was in a heavy, dense forest. A mountain stream ran through the middle of the field, flowing to the south. A small bridge in the center of the field crossed the stream.

Tero's army, waiting near their campsite, readied themselves. Tero's spies informed him a dragon was spotted in the area but was nowhere to be found now.

"Keep a lookout for that dragon. It must be defeated first. The dragon is the key to victory," Tero reminded his commanders.

"Nicola must be killed. We will not take her prisoner," a rage-filled Tero demanded to the whole army.

As Tero paced back and forth, an arrow flew from the eastern forest and struck his top general in the heart.

"Fire into the forest!" yelled Tero. A volley of shots was fired into the forest. A second arrow, this time from the western woods, struck another general that was next to Tero. This time the arrow was in the general's back. "They are surrounding us," surprisingly said Tero to his third and last general.

"What are your orders, Sire?" the general pleaded.

Tero, with no hesitation or emotion, answered, "Burn the forest. That will draw them out of the woods. Our guns will be ready when they flee from the fire."

A blazing fire was set, and the forest started to smoke. Soon after, a raging fire was going. Some of Nicola's army ran toward the western gate to get to the ruins; others ran south and made their way to the western side. Others ran out to the field to the waiting ambush by Tero's army. Nicola watched in horror as the soldiers fell one by one.

Nicola quickly decided that something had to be done. Her army was no match for Tero and his army. She nodded toward Karisma, and the two decided to use their magic. They combined to create a mist that covered the field. It was a like a very dense fog. As the mist settled on Tero's army, arrows started flying from the unburning woods. Elek, frown with fear, slowly snuck his way to the stream and hid under the bridge. Tero's army was terrified as the mist came and arrows started to rain down on them. Some of them started to scatter to save their lives. Nothing like this had ever happened before to an army of Silvager.

Tero laughed at his misfortune and told his general, "This is a trick caused by Nicola. Very clever, but it will not last long."

A few minutes later, Nicola's magic started to fade. Karisma used the opportunity to change into the dragon and destroy all the big weapons with one blast of fire. As the fireball exploded the weapons, Nicola changed back into her human form; unfortunately, since she was still new at using magic, she was directly next to Tero when she changed back. Tero smiled at his change of fortune. He threw her to the ground and held her down with his foot until he could tie her hands behind her back. Nicola struggled to get on her knees.

Tero looked at her and laughed, saying, "Do you still think that you can beat me? There are things that you do not even know about." Tero kicked Nicola in the ribs, and she fell back on the ground. "Fire the dragon weapon!"

A loud explosion sounded from the northern woods. A couple seconds later, Karisma was trapped in a net and crashed into the field. The more she struggled, the tighter the net became.

"You cannot beat me, Nicola." Tero glared and shoved her back to the ground as she struggled back to her knees. "You will see your army get defeated, then you will die. I gave you a chance to be my slave, and you answered by killing my brother."

Nicola looked up at Tero with great fear in her eyes. Karisma was captured. Her army was trying to flee, only met with the sounds of muskets firing. She felt like she failed as a queen.

"What should we do with the dragon?" Tero was asked by his last general.

"Lock her up. She is full of magic. This beast will help me in ruling the island. We must thank Nicola for this gift," answered Tero while he shoved her back to the ground.

Tero, looking down Nicola, mocked, "Nicola, I was hoping this battle would be longer. My army has been bored, and we were looking for a longer fight. Sonoma was no match, and you have been nothing to us." More gunshots were heard in the western woods. "I believe your army is almost gone. Your kingdom is gone. Your parents are gone. You now have *nothing* left."

Some of Tero's army was busy loading Karisma into a cart to haul her back to Tilton.

"Look over there. Your pet dragon has been captured, and it cannot help. I do not hear any more gunfire. It sounds like your army is gone. Do you want to die here, or do you want me to take you back to where your palace once stood?" Tero arrogantly mocked Nicola with a kick to the ribs again.

Nicola looked toward the field, this time with tears in her eyes. *I am sorry, Father and Mother. I failed you,* she thought to herself. Then she saw one of the soldiers making his way toward Tero, carrying a large sword.

Tero looked into Nicola's blue eyes and raised his sword to her heart. He pulled the sword back, and with one quick motion, he pierced Nicola's heart. Nicola fell over and took her last breath in the middle of the field.

"You there, how is the battle going? Are they all dead?" asked Tero to the approaching soldier.

As Nicola fell, the soldier sprinted to Tero.

"I do not know," he said.

Tero looked confused, "Who are you?"

The soldier swung his longsword and slashed Tero's head. As the sword struck Tero, the soldier's helmet fell off.

The soldier replied, "I am Elek, the savior of Nicola."

Elek looked down at Nicola as Tero collapsed. Elek kneeled down and held Nicola in his arms and cried out loud. A golden flash of light came out of Nicola and surrounded the battlefield. Both armies, seeing that Nicola and Tero were dead, stopped fighting and dropped their weapons. Karisma was untied. She finally could change back to her human form, and then she ran as fast as she could to Nicola.

"She is gone," said a choked-up and teary-eyed Elek. "This is not how it is supposed to end, or is it?"

Karisma softly cried and said, "No, this is not the destiny that I was taught. There is one way that we can save her."

"How?" tearfully asked Elek. "She is dead."

"Yes, but there is a flower which can save her. It is located inside the hot springs of Desert Springs," replied Karisma.

"Can you take me there to save Nicola's life?" asked Elek with some hope coming back in his voice.

Karisma said, "I will go alone. This is a quest that only I can perform. You need to take Nicola's body back to Unidade. I will meet you there."

Karisma changed into the dragon and took flight. Elek found an empty cart and gently loaded Nicola's body into it. He walked slowly to Unidade. As he walked past each soldier, each one would lower their sword and bow their head. Then they would follow in tribute to their fallen queen. Tero's last remaining general grabbed the cart and helped Elek on his journey.

Karisma flew straight to the hot springs as fast as her wings could carry her. The trip took her about five minutes. She circled around the springs three times while angrily saying something to Ulric the Wizard, and she then dove straight into the middle of the hot springs about two hundred feet. There she found a cave with a red light radiantly glowing out of the entrance.

Karisma swam into the entrance of the cave. The cave entrance was about one hundred feet long. The glowing light looked to be coming from the top of the tunnel. When she got to the cave entrance, the water suddenly was gone, and an empty cave was in front of her. The red light glowed in front of her. She changed back into her human form and walked toward the far end of the room, where the light was coming from.

The glowing light was coming from the wall of the room. Karisma looked at the wall and found some symbols carved in the rock walls. The symbols showed a flower and an island rising out of the water. Another symbol showed a lake and a tower. A third symbol showed a dead girl holding a flower.

Karisma waved her hand over the symbols, and the wall slowly opened to show the most beautiful flower. It was a glowing red color with midnight-blue petals. Karisma pulled one of the twelve petals off. She waved her hand over the flower, and the wall slowly closed to cover the flower. A new symbol appeared on the wall. The new picture showed what looked like Karisma saving Nicola. Karisma smiled at this and made her way back to the Unidade.

"Thank you, Ulric,' she said as she left the cave.

Elek made his way to Unidade. All the soldiers and townspeople followed him in deep silence. All their heads were lowered in sadness for the loss of their beloved Nicola. Elek took the cart to the entrance of the tombs. He looked at Nicola's body, and then he glanced up toward the sky. In the distance, he could see a dragon flying toward him. The dragon was holding something that was glowing red. Elek couldn't make out what the object was, but it was glowing brightly in the now-rising moon.

Karisma landed and changed back into her human form once again.

"Quickly bring her into the tomb," she commanded to Elek.

Karisma followed Elek into the tomb. A minute later, Elek left the tomb, protesting all the way out. One of the soldiers handed a sword to Elek, the sword of Tero. Elek accepted the gift with a smile.

Thirty painfully slow minutes went by. The crowd looked at Elek for answers to what was going on, but he had no answers for them. Then Karisma slowly exited the tombs followed a minute later by Nicola. Nicola gave a huge smile to the waiting crowd and ran to Elek to give him a kiss, a kiss that became a legend on the island.

"The battle is over, just like destiny said," Karisma exclaimed. "Tero's army never wanted to fight the battle, but they fought out of the fear of the rage of Tero. Nicola, now you can unite the island to bring peace once and for all."

"What is your command, my queen?" Tero's general said to Nicola. He took off his helmet and bowed his head.

Nicola gave them a speech, talking about forgiving each other for the battle that took place. She also talked about not forgetting what the lust for power would do, using the examples of Caelon and Tero. She urged everyone to join her; to unify the island and help the island become what it once was before the corruptions took place. The people cheered her as she spoke with great authority and courage. Unfortunately, for us, the words were never written down for the future generations to read.

After the speech, the commanders of both armies crowned Nicola the queen of the island. Karisma waved her hand, and a crown appeared. It was made of white gold and had the shape of three flower stems that were loosely wrapped around and met into one glorious golden flower on the front. "All hail, Nicola," was heard as she accepted the crown. Grown men cried at the events they witnessed that day.

CHAPTER 41

Nicola's First Command

Nicola looked at the crowd and bowed to them with humbleness and humility. The crowd, surprised with her actions, cheered for their new queen.

She glanced at Elek and said, "My first command as your queen is to rescue the slaves of Silvager. No person should be put through that life. Elek, your son will be returned to you. Everyone who lost a child to Tero, your child will be returned."

She grabbed Tero's sword out of Elek's hand and turned around and looked at Karisma. Karisma smiled at her and changed into the dragon. Nicola climbed on and the two flew off to Tilton to find the slaves.

"You have to be careful in Tilton. Many of Tero's men do not know the events that transpired today and will still be loyal to Tero."

Nicola shook her head in agreement.

A few minutes passed, and Karisma landed near Tilton. They could see what looked like mines going into the hills, but they needed a closer look to confirm their thoughts. Karisma changed into her human form, and the two walked quietly through the trees to get a better look. The trees were thick and made hiding easy. Nicola moved some branches so she could see better, and what she saw horrified her.

A large man wearing a Silvagerian battle suit, one that almost matched Tero's, stood holding a braided whip. Children were running in and out of the mine, just like ants running in and out of their hole. The children were carrying tools, pushing carts, and doing whatever else the guard was yelling at them. She held back the tears from seeing the children suffer.

Karisma looked into Nicola's eyes and said, "I will use magic to distract the guard so you can get inside of the mine. I do not know what lies inside. Everything you need to succeed is inside you. Use what you have learned. Be brave, be strong, you are the hope of the children."

Karisma disappeared and reappeared as a vapor of blue mist over the guard's head. The guard was confused and waved his hands over his face, trying to remove the mist that blocked his vision. Nicola sprinted with all her might into the entrance of the mine. The children looked confused and happy at the same time, seeing an adult not holding a whip in their hand.

"Where are the rest of you?" Nicola politely asked one of the children. "I am here to free all of you. You will no longer be slaves on this island. The entrance is opened and ready for you to leave."

The scared and staved-looking child answered, "At the end of the mine. Be careful. There are soldiers down there guarding one of the children. I heard his dad is wanted by King Tero."

"Tero is dead. His army was defeated today in Aurumton. I am Nicola, the new queen, and I will not allow slaves on my island," Nicola corrected the boy.

"If this is true, good luck to you," the boy said, and he ran as fast as he could to the opened entrance.

The other children saw the boy run out and soon followed his lead.

Nicola walked down the mine shaft and near the end and could see five guards surrounding one boy. She could make out a couple of sentences the guards said.

One asked, "Where are the rest of the children? They should have been back by now. I am going to check on them."

A second guard said something, and the two of them walked toward Nicola.

She slowly, trying not to make a sound, drew her sword. The guards looked at each other and mumbled something as they walked toward Nicola. One of the guards walked throat-first into the sword and fell to his knees. The second guard grabbed his sword and pointed it at Nicola.

The two jousted for what felt like hours. Nicola's skill equaled the guard's strength. In the middle of the long battle, the guard noticed something.

"You are a criminal. You have stolen King Tero's sword. The penalty for being a thief is death. Even for beautiful girls such as you. Maybe we can reach a deal. You can be my slave, work here under my watch, and I can give the king his sword back."

Nicola rolled her eyes, dodged a swing of the sword, and sternly answered back, "I am your queen. Tero lost the battle today. You can surrender and bow to your new queen, or you can spend the rest of your days in prison."

"Tero's powerful army could never lose to Nicola's pathetic band of misfits. I would be more powerful than anything she could find," the guard boasted and weakly swung his sword at Nicola.

Nicola smiled and said, "You are getting tired fighting with 'a girl.' If you are so powerful, then why are you here in a mine babysitting one child?"

Nicola swung her sword with great might, and the guard's sword broke into three pieces.

The guard had no answers for Nicola, and he sprinted out of the mine toward Tilton, never to be seen again. Nicola thought to herself, *Two down, three more to go.* She rested for a few minutes before she went to see the last three guards.

"Hello, boys," Nicola flirted as she walked to the end of the mine tunnel.

The guards looked shocked to see a woman in the mine.

One of them asked, "Who are you, you lovely lady?"

"I am your queen. Tero has been defeated." The guards laughed. "We can do this the easy way, or we can do this the hard way," she spoke softly. She looked at Elek's son and said, "Your father killed Tero. I am here to set you free."

"Do not listen to her boy," one of the guards snapped. He whipped the boy twice with his whip. "She is lying to you. You know your father is weak and spineless."

The boy cried out in pain. Nicola lifter her sword and struck the guard's hand. The hand and whip fell to the ground.

The guard grabbed his arm and kneeled on his left knee, saying, "Get her. She will pay for this crime against Tero and his army."

A few minutes later, the guard fell over.

"This is your last chance. Surrender your weapons. The battle is over. The island is one. Peace now reigns. Tero's rage is over," Nicola pleaded.

The smallest of the three guards dropped his sword and ran to his home in Tilton.

The other guard raised his sword to Nicola's heart and said, "You will pay for crimes. Spreading this blasphemy is punishable by death in Silvager. I don't know where you came from, but your stupid-sounding voice tells me it is not Silvager. You will die in the town center so everyone knows your crime."

Nicola laughed and swung her sword at the guard. The swords clashed with giants sparks in the dark tunnel. The battle raged for five minutes. The guard, using his size and strength, pinned Nicola against the wall.

"I should kiss you. A girl of your beauty shouldn't be wasted," the guard, smiling, bragged. "A kiss, then I will kill you for your crimes against our king."

Nicola closed her eyes and remembered what Karisma told her. She took a slow and deep breath and changed into the golden mist. The guard leaned to kiss her and kissed the wall of the tunnel instead. He looked surprised and turned to see what happened. Nicola quickly changed back to her human form and grabbed his sword in her free hand.

She pointed both swords at the guard and said, "Death should come to those who refuse to obey their queen, but I am not a tyrant like the ones before." She tied his hands behind his back and commanded, "You shall live, but the dungeon shall be your home. I will not kill out of anger."

She looked at Elek's son, and with a great gentleness, he was untied and set free.

"Your father was very brave today. He killed Tero and saved me," she whispered to him.

She gave him a small kiss on the cheek. The kiss was met with a giant blushing face.

The three of them walked out the tunnel to meet Karisma, who was still surrounding the large guard with the mist. She changed into her human form, and the guard was confused, seeing the boy, two ladies, and one of his guards in front of him.

"It is all right. Drop your whip and come with us. No harm will happen to you," Nicola firmly commanded.

Karisma waved her hand, and the guard lost all memories of why he was there. She clapped her hands, and the guard that was tied up appeared in the dungeon, never to be heard or seen again.

"Um. Okay," the guard said, still dazed from what just happened.

Karisma changed into the dragon. The boy and guard were a little scared but climbed on anyway. They flew back to Unidade and met with the people of the island once again.

Elek ran to them as they landed and grabbed his son and gave him a large bear hug. Nicola joined in the hug a few minutes later.

CHAPTER 42

Nicola's Reign

Much of the records writing of Nicola's reign were destroyed. Only a few things remain that were passed down from person to person. The most important thing that she was remembered was that she was the most just, honorable, and peaceful ruler of the island. Her first order as queen was to release all the slaves in Silvager. Elek child would come home to live in the palace this time. Then she ordered that the people destroy the palaces in Tilton and Facultas. She did not want the memories of greed and the lust for power to remain. She then ordered that a new palace was to be built in Unidade, next to the tombs of the three brothers. Nicola wanted her palace to be located where the first capital was located, a promise she made to Karisma earlier.

When the palace was completed a year later, she married Elek on her twentieth birthday. She wanted the first event of the new palace to be a special occasion. Over time, the new king and queen would have five children, two boys and two girls of their own, along with Nicola's stepson. Years later, each child would grow up, get married, and have many children of their own. Nicola would have twenty grandchildren. She loved spending time with each one of them, taking time to read books and teach them about the magic of the island.

Nicola also built a memorial for her parents. The monument was placed in Aurumton City, where the palace once stood. She visited there often.

Karisma, who never aged due to the curse of the wizard, stayed with Nicola and Elek, helping where she could.

Nicola reigned as queen for almost seventy peaceful years. The whole island prospered during her reign. All the people mourned her death at the age of eighty-eight. Karisma thought about the flower but decided that Nicola had done her job.

Her final command as queen was to have two of her granddaughters become queens and rule together. Maybe at another time, Nicola would be needed. Until then, Karisma would continue to watch over Nicola's family

PART IV

History after Nicola

Not much is known about this time in history. Nicola named her twin granddaughters, Jadyn and Chelsea, to be queens of the island. They were known as the last of the great rulers of the island. Nicola's choice of rulers would cause bitterness between the three kingdoms of the island. The bitterness that tore them apart caused the recorded history to disappear. As each generation grew older, the bitterness grew, causing the people to grow apart once more.

Six generations had now passed since Nicola ruled over the island with great honor and dignity. As the people of the island grew further apart from each other, each kingdom would become separate from each other once again, and the kingdom would once again appoint their own ruler. The central capital city of Unidade became a lost city to the people, and the island's magic was lost once more. Karisma, worried about the survival of the island, hid in her tower, not to be seen after Jadyn's and Chelsea's rule ended. Karisma became a long-forgotten memory of the people as time went on.

Each ruler became fiercer than the one before them. Battles started to happen over what was left of the resources of each kingdom. Soon the island was stripped of all its glorious resources. The magnificent forests of Silvager were gone, never to grow toward the great blue sky again. The natural resources, which the kingdom once offered to the island, were used well beyond their capacities. The fertile fields of Insidiaville were dried up once more, nothing more than dust. The great farms that Nicola restored were lost and never able to produce the much-needed food the people longed for. The peaceful flowing and majestic river, which divided Insidiaville and Aurumton, was all dried up and left begging for any trickle of water that could be spared. The great gold mines of Aurumton were destroyed during a battle and then sealed, never to be opened and mined again. The island had lost everything that it offered to the people. Death was everywhere, and people begged for a hero.

Karisma would watch the destruction happen from her tower. Each time the island lost, her magic would become less. The last thing she worried about was the hot springs in Insidiaville, the source of the island's magic. The only thing that kept her magic going was that the hot springs were still bubbling. The magic that gave the water its healing touch was left untouched. She hoped that someone would be worthy to save the island one more time.

CHAPTER 43

Karisma's Hopelessness

Karisma sat in her tower, longing for the days of old, the day of Nicola's reign. She would watch the sun rise and set over the lake each day and wonder how people could become so corrupted in their own personal quest for power and riches instead of repeating the past mistakes. She hoped that the people of the island could just sit and watch, as she and King Cass did. Such beauty was missed every day. The island would talk to them, she knew it.

She also had many worries that she would think of each day. The magic was almost all used up. She had very little magic left for her to use. What she had was not enough to fix the island one more time. The island's magic was almost gone due to the ongoing corruptness of the kingdoms. The island had no way to take care of itself. Nothing could grow, and if it did, it would not survive. The loss of everything made people more aggressive toward their rival kingdoms. They wanted what they did not have.

The battles became more frequent, and each battle led to greater violence. With each battle, the island's people became less numerous. With no resources available, it became harder to repopulate the island. The armies would take younger boys each time, leaving no one to work at home. The population was small, and Karisma feared the end of the people was near. Only the once-spectacular capital cities that were rebuilt after Nicola passed away remained, but not close to their former glory.

As the people became more and more desperate in their search for anything they could use, Karisma became worried that the lost city of Unidade would be found. The tombs of the three brothers and the tomb of Nicola were located there. Karisma did not want the tombs to be disturbed because it was a place of great honor to the great kings and queen of the past. She used some of her little magic to seal and hide the tombs from ever being found and disturbed by anyone. Nicola and the three brothers did not deserve to be used for political gain.

Karisma also hid Kingsbridge Lake and her tower from the people of the island. She did not want these to be found. Karisma watched as the people desecrated their kingdoms, and she was afraid of what the people would do to her lake. Kingsbridge Lake was the last place of true beauty on the island, and Karisma not only needed it to stay that way, but she wanted it to stay to remind her of what once was.

Karisma felt hopeless as the island became less each day. She longed for the days of her brothers, the three kings that ruled justly and with great honor together, and for the days of Nicola. Queen Nicola was the only one to rule over three kingdoms, something that no one in history had ever done. She did it with such grace and honor it could never be repeated. Back in the past, the island kept and refilled its magic, the people loved their rulers, and Karisma's magic could do anything she wanted. The people would work with the island, not against it.

Tears fell from her eyes as she looked at the brilliant sunset and thought. As she cried, a violent windstorm battered the coast of Insidiaville.

CHAPTER 44

A Hope Arrives

The people on the island needed help with basic needs, and their kings and queens could do nothing to aid them. The people heard stories of a great and powerful lady that would help the people in the past, but that was all they were to them, just handed-down stories. The people were hungry and needed help to find food because the fields, water, and forests were gone. They needed help to build houses because their mighty trees were gone. They needed protection from the other kingdoms, and since the population of the island had dramatically decreased, no kingdom had anyone left for an army. They had nowhere to turn. People begged for hope.

One day a small boat gently landed on the sandy shores of Insidiaville. An old and oddly familiar man got out and looked around. He was around five feet tall and wore a robe of scarlet red and black. The robe was long and just touched the ground as he stood. The robe was lined with small images of wolves. The back of the robe was black and had a picture of a red moon with a wolf's face inside. His face was old, wrinkled, and clean. His eyes were small and looked black. He had a long white beard that matched his long white hair. He carried a dark black staff in his left haft hand.

He looked around and said in his tired and raspy-sounding voice, "I have found the island after hundreds of years of looking for it."

The old man left to find the nearest city, which was Facultas, the battered capital of Insidiaville.

When he reached the city, he saw many poor people begging for anything that could be given to them. He needed to find some young men, men that would be able to do the work that he needed to be done. The old man decided to look for the tavern, thinking that drunken men would be easy to persuade to get his much-needed help.

He saw a group of five young men at a table. They looked dirty and rough.

"How are you boys doing on this fine day? I have a proposition for you. Do you care to listen?" the old man quietly asked.

The strongest-looking man looked up and said, "What do you have, old man? Make it quick. Our beer is getting warmer."

The group chuckled at his comment. He stood around six feet tall and had short and curly red hair. His face was covered in lots of freckles. His eyes were dark green and almost glowed in the firelight. He sounded like he was from Scotland when he spoke. He claimed to be a direct descendant of Caelon, but his friends always laughed at his claim. He claimed the kingdom should be his, but his time searching through the historical archives ended with Caelon's defeat to Tero.

The old man firmly stated, "Meet me on the south shore at sunset, and *I* will make it worth your time."

He glared at the five men, turned around, and walked out of the tavern.

The five men blankly looked at each other.

"Should we go?" asked one of them.

"We will. We have nothing to lose. If he has nothing to offer us, his staff and robe will be worth some money. At least we will be able to get more beer," the strong redheaded one said.

A few hours later, as the sun set, the men found the old man on the shore.

"What do you want from us," the big, red, and strong man asked sarcastically.

The old man quietly answered and waved his hand, "Come with me, alone, and we will talk. I know who you are, and I know you are the 'leader' of your group."

"I am Gulaga, and what you mean, you know who I am?" questioned Gulaga with a puzzled look.

The old man answered, "You are the rightful king of Insidiaville. Caelon had an affair when he was married to Nicola because he despised her greatly. You are the only descendant of Cass's line alive today. Your line in history was erased from history to keep what honor, which was not a lot, of Caelon intact."

Gulaga answered excitedly, "I knew it. I want to make my *friends* bow to me."

"Don't get involved with that. I have a way to make you powerful and rich beyond any of your dreams. After you become wealthy, then worry about establishing your rightful kingdom," the old man scolded.

"Rich and powerful? How can you do that? This island has nothing left," Gulaga persisted.

The old man snickered and said, "You are wrong. There is one thing the island has that the people of the world want. They want the water from the hot springs of the ruins of Desert Springs. You and your friends get me the water, and I will pay you greatly for it," calmly answered the old man. "The so-called kings and queens of this pitiful island will be bowing down to you."

"Money and riches? I am in," exclaimed Gulaga.

The two new friends parted ways. Gulaga reported to his friends the details of the conversation, leaving out the part of his relation to Caelon until another day. They all went back to the tavern for the night, excited for the next morning to come.

The five of them arrived early the next morning.

"How do we get the water out of the hot springs? We have nothing to put it in and no way to get it out," Gulaga asked with minor arrogance in his voice.

The old man looked at the water and tapped his staff on the shore. Bottles appeared. A few moments later, a machine appeared, a machine with water-catching pouches which could easily fill the bottles. The machine had three large wheels in a triangular shape. A belt that held the pouches moved around the large wheels. A small wheel between two of the large wheels controlled the speed.

The men went to work filling the bottles with the magical water. The work was easy and boring at times. Each time they would fill one hundred bottles, the old man would hit his staff on the ground. The bottles would disappear, and five bags of gold would appear. The men loved this easy job because they loved the money.

After six months of filling bottles, a dome-shaped cave could be seen in the center of the hot springs.

"What is in the cave?" asked Gulaga with the sense that secrets were not being shared.

"When the water is completely gone, we will find out," the old man firmly answered.

Each day passed, and less water was available to fill the bottles. After a year, the water was gone. The men were sad that they would not get any more bags of gold, but they were the five richest men on the island. Kings and queens begged to know where they got the money, but none of them would tell.

The last day came of getting the water, and the old man challenged them, "How would you like to double all of the gold you made?"

"What would you like us to do?" Gulaga asked with a greediness that had not been seen since Caelon.

The old man answered, "Go in the cave and retrieve the item in the center of it."

Gulaga arrogantly asked, "What item?"

The man glared, and his eyes turned a fiery red.

"You will know this item when you see it. I will leave you, and I will be back in a few days. When I get the item, I will double your gold. I am going to search for a lady."

"As you command," the excited men said.

The old man left, and the five men went on their adventure to the cave. Climbing down the banks was slow and dangerous. One of the men slipped and fell to his death. The other four continued on their way. They reached the bottom of the springs and looked up toward the entrance of the cave, but there was no way to get there. The cliff was too steep, and the rocks were too slippery to even try to the climb. They decided to wait and let the rocks dry a bit longer, hoping that would help in their quest.

The old man wandered around for three days and found nothing.

"I know she is here. I can feel her magic. Where are you Karisma? I am here for your island. Come to me."

CHAPTER 45

Inside the Cave

Karisma secretly watched as the water left the hot springs. Her eyes filled with fear. She watched the five men as they left to search the cave. She stayed still and hidden as the old man looked for her. The old man looked very familiar to her, yet she never recalled meeting him. Inside he felt to her like a nightmare or a horrific vision she once saw. She wanted to use her magic to find out who the mysterious old man was, but it the magic was extremely limited as the water left the hot springs. She needed to find help, and she needed it fast. There was only one way she knew how to get help, using the flower in the cave—the same flower that created the island and the same flower that brought Nicola back to life, also the same flower she instructed the brothers never to touch. She was sure the flower could help her one more time.

Karisma quickly made the decision to get the flower before the men could find a way to reach the cave. She used what was left of her magic to change into a dragon and fly to the cave. With a blue puff of mist, she took flight and was off on her quest. She flew past the old man on her way toward the cave.

The old man smiled as he looked up and saw Karisma flying by.

"I found you," he marveled as he slowly turned back and headed toward the hot springs. "You will retrieve the flower, and it will be mine." He laughed at his hope of good fortune.

Karisma darted past the four men, taking only a second to launch a large fireball at them. The fireball struck the men and burned them instantly. Their bodies turned to ash and drifted into the mud. She turned her flight up to the entrance of the cave and landed with grace and elegance as she changed back into her human form. She felt saddened in heart for killing the four men, but she had to protect the flower at all costs. After all, Goran was almost banned from a made-up trial for retrieving the flower.

Karisma, feeling weak from using her magic, limped into the cave and down the hall toward the great sealed door. The pictures on the sealed door changed from a person being saved with a flower to a picture of a flower. Karisma once again waved her hand, and the door opened. The chamber behind the door contained the beautiful, glowing midnight-blue flower with a red center. Karisma picked up the flower just as the old man appeared in the room.

"Karisma, give me the flower. It is now mine," he commanded.

Karisma looked at the man with fear in her eyes, a fear she never felt before. It felt to her like she was going to lose everything, and there was nothing she could do to stop it. Holding the flower close to her helped her regain some of the lost magic. She changed herself back into the dragon and flew as fast as she could to the tombs of Unidade. As she flew off, the old man threw his staff in her direction. The staff fell near the cave entrance without any harm to anything.

"I will get that flower," he vowed with all the vengeance in his heart.

Karisma landed at the entrance of the tombs and once again changed back into her human form. The flower glowed brighter, and Karisma's magic grew strong. The tombs were covered with moss and thorn-covered ivy. Behind the ivy was an inscription that read, "The great kings and queen forever rest here." She waved her hand over the sealed tombs, and the stone instantly crumbled to small pebbles. She walked in the tomb and placed the flower in the center of the main room.

The flower glowed, like the full moon on a cloudless night, and lit the entire place. Karisma could see the tombs of the great kings and queen of the past. Tears welled up in her eyes as she remembered each of them. She knelt on her right knee and waved her hand over the flower.

The walls shook violently, and the tombs of the three brothers crumbled into dust.

"Karisma!" was heard from the middle tomb.

Karisma looked toward the voice and said, "It is good to see you, Goran."

Goran walked away from the rubble, followed by his brothers, Salem and Cass, each looking like the day they became kings of the island.

The walls started to shake more violently. Karisma and the brothers held each other, trying to keep pieces of stone from hitting them as the walls shook. A thunderous collapse was heard, and dust and dirt made a cloud. When the cloud settled, the four of them turned around and saw a beautiful blond lady standing with a giant smile.

"Karisma, my friend!" said the lady, "What has happened that you need us?"

"Nicola!" said Karisma. "I missed you, my friend." The two gave each other a big hug and laughed with the joy of seeing each other once again. "Each of you has been restored to what you were when you became rulers of the island. I need your help in stopping a new evil, one that threatens the very existence of the island."

"What do you need us to do?" Nicola asked with the innocence of a child.

The floor started shaking violently, like a large earthquake, and from the dirt an old man appeared, wearing a midnight-blue robe.

"Ulric," said a surprised Karisma.

"In the flesh," Ulric said, and he bowed to the kings and queen of old.

"All of your prophecies that you told me have come true. The three brothers, Cass, Salem, and Goran, ruled together. Nicola brought the island back together. There is a new evil. An old man wearing a scarlet-red robe threatens the island. This is something that you did not tell me. I don't know what to do, and I need your help.

I need help from all of you," begged Karisma, using her eyes to help in her begging.

After they all greeted each other, Karisma began to cry.

"What's wrong?" questioned a concerned Nicola.

"I always dreamed of the day that we would all be together, but I was hoping that it would be under happy times. Not an island that lost everything," Karisma explained.

"We will do what we can to make things right again," said Cass "The island will be back to the way it was."

Karisma half smiled at Cass, trying to hide how bad things really were.

CHAPTER 46

The Old Man

Ulric looked at Karisma and asked, "Tell me about this old man."

Karisma started to tell the story of the events of the island after the rule of Jadyn and Chelsea but was interrupted by Goran.

"Can you start from when we three brothers died since we haven't heard the story of my granddaughter?"

Karisma smiled and restarted from then. She told the story of Nicola and Elek and how they stopped Caelon and Tero.

Goran interrupted once more, "I knew my kin would be great!"

Karisma quieted Goran by waving her hand, causing Goran to place his hand over his own mouth, and then she continued by telling of Jadyn and Chelsea, and they were the last of the great rulers of the island. Karisma told how to island lost everything it has to offer. She then told how the old man got on to the island. She told how the old man had five men empty the hot springs of the magical water. She ended with the men and old man trying to get the flower.

Ulric looked concerned. He waved his hand above his head, and an image appeared in the mist of the old man.

"The old man is my twin brother, Alva Thoth. I banished him before the island was created. He has come looking to rule the world by using this flower. There was more to the prophecy than I told you."

Karisma looked surprised when Ulric told her there was more and said, "You didn't tell me the whole prophecy?"

"The end of times is now upon the island," Ulric replied without hesitation.

He rubbed his hands together, knowing that he could not hide anything from the group.

Turning pale with fear, like the rest of her friends, Karisma asked, "End of times?"

Ulric continued, "Long, long ago, both Alva Thoth and I were wizards in the nomad wolf tribe. Our magic balanced us together. I liked creating, and he likes destroying. Together we were one. Separate, one had too much power. Alva Thoth, much like Az Rex, lusted for power, and when we heard of the flower, his lust for greater power took over. I had him banished to an isolated mountain in the middle of the world, and I went on a quest to find this flower. When I learned of the location of the flower, it was a place that I could not reach. I made a deal with a king and queen—your parents, Karisma—to obtain the flower. I created this island to keep the flower safe. It was safe for over seven hundred years, until now. Alva Thoth will not stop until he gets what he wants. My magic could only keep Alva Thoth prisoned for the seven hundred years. Good had control for those years, and to balance the good, evil must control the flower for seven hundred years."

"If he has the flower, then he has the island?" quietly questioned Salem.

Ulric responded with great sadness, "Yes, that is correct."

Goran, never wanting to back down from a challenge, said, "We will find a way to stop him. My brothers found a way to save me from my isolation and punishment. I know that we can stop this new evil from taking our island."

Cass smiled and jokingly replied, "Just don't kill me this time."

The brothers and Karisma laughed while Nicola looked lost with the conversation, but she giggled in the background.

"Does Alva Thoth have a weakness?" asked Goran while trying to plot in his head.

Ulric sincerely replied, "Only his lust for power. He is a great wizard, greater than I. He is extremely strong and will stop and nothing to obtain the flower and the island."

"He needs what we have," calmly replied Salem while looking at the flower.

"Can't we just seal the flower in this tomb? It will be protected by all of us inside of here," questioned Nicola.

Ulric shook his head and replied, "We cannot. Alva Thoth will not stop at a sealed tomb. He is a very powerful wizard, more powerful than anyone can imagine. He can feel the flower's power as he gets closer. The closer he gets to the flower, the more powerful he will become. A sealed tomb will not be able to stop him. It will slow him down for a few moments, but it will never stop him."

"We can stand up and fight," eagerly stated Goran, grabbing the golden handle of his long silver sword. "No one has been able to match my strength, and an old man will not beat me."

"We can, but Alva Thoth is stronger than you realize. His might does not come from strength. He can manipulate anyone to help him. He got the five men to do the work at the hot springs, he can find more people to fight all of us" rebuked Ulric.

"We were once all rulers of this island. Won't anyone listen to us? There have to be stories floating around of how we ruled before the island lost everything. Nicola was the greatest, and she did it against great odds. The people have to believe in the impossible once again. Karisma taught us this before. She can do it again," begged Salem.

Ulric looked at him and sadly said, "They are like you stated, just stories of the past. All have become lost in time or just a fairy tale to the small number of people left on the island. The people don't believe in the past anymore. There is no hope in the future, and Karisma can do nothing to restore their lost hope. All they have seen is the bad times. No one believes good can ever happen."

Nicola tearfully looked at Karisma and cried with her heart, "You helped me when events went wrong. We beat Tero's powerful army, and you saved my life in the process. I will find a way to help you, my old friend." She embraced Karisma and let go a few minutes later.

Nicola's eyes light up as she spoke to the group, "I agree with Goran. We will make our stand here in the tomb. Alva Thoth doesn't know that we are here. He only knows of Karisma. We have the advantage. We will take down Alva Thoth now. Each of us has been through tough times. I have heard the old stories of the brothers and the older stories of Ulric. I have my own story of pain and triumph. Together we are powerful, and Alva Thoth will not know what hit him. Let's use this advantage and stop this new evil from taking what we made glorious."

The group excitedly agreed, all except Ulric who kept warning of Alva Thoth's strength. Ulric walked to the entrance of the tomb and waved his hand. The entrance shut and sealed itself. After Ulric made sure the cave was sealed tightly, he sat down and mediated about the upcoming battle.

CHAPTER 47

Alva Thoth's Search

Alva Thoth slowly walked into the main chamber of the cave. He looked in and could see nothing since the glowing flower was gone. He waved his hand over his staff, and it lit up, just like a bright torch. He walked into the main room of the cave and looked around the empty room. The sealed wall where the flower once grew was still opened. Some dirt fell off the roots and was left in place of the flower.

Alva Thoth grabbed the dirt and grumbled, "Much power is in the flower. I can feel the powerful magic in the dirt that held the flower."

Alva Thoth changed into a red glowing wolf and ran out of the cave, leaped over the now-empty hot spring to the sandy shore, and sped toward the mountains. A deafening howl was heard across the island as Alva Thoth reached the top of the rocky pass. He looked down the opposite side of the pass and could see the top of Karisma's tower.

Alva Thoth ran full speed to the tower in search of Karisma. The magical door that protected Karisma was no match for the strength of Alva Thoth. He darted through the door and straight up the stairs and changed back into the old man.

"Where are you?" he said.

There was no answer. Alva Thoth looked through Karisma's room for anything that could help him. He felt a vision, one of Tero and the fight with Nicola. He had another vision, one that showed him the hidden tomb of Unidade. He also saw Nicola and brothers protecting Karisma.

"You thought you could be sneaky and try to stop me with the help of your old friends. That is not going to work. The flower will be mine, and you and your friends will be gone forever."

He raised his hands toward the sky, and a bright-red flash of lightning struck the tower, and it disintegrated into smoking dust. Nothing was left of the once-symbolic tower of the island.

Alva Thoth made a plan of what he wanted to do.

"I want to make Karisma suffer as much as I have, being isolated for seven hundred years," he calmly said to the dust of the tower.

He changed into a dark-red misty cloud, and a quick moment later, he appeared in Silvager. There he searched for the grave of Tero, the short-lived mighty king of Silvager. Once he found the grave, he slammed his staff on the head of the grave. Tero rose out of it.

"Who are you? Why would you summon me out of my forever slumber?" questioned Tero.

"I am Alva Thoth, the mighty and great wizard of the wolf tribe. I created you five hundred years ago to complete a quest, and now I need you to finish that quest. Kill Nicola, make her suffer the fate of death. I want Karisma to suffer hard, and when Nicola suffers, Karisma suffers," answered Alva Thoth.

Tero looked surprised and said, "Didn't I kill her before? I felt her die as my sword struck her heart."

"Yes, she died, but Karisma brought her back. Karisma used magic, and Nicola was alive then and is alive now, and I want you to kill her one more time. Make her suffer. As she suffers, Karisma suffers." Alva Thoth laughed as he spoke.

Tero smiled and replied, "I will kill her, but I want to rule this island after."

Alva Thoth, looking at Tero sternly, said, "I *will rule the world*, but you can be the king of this island. You will bow to me, but you can have the island."

Tero happily agreed to the terms that Alva Thoth offered, and the two started to make their way to the lost tombs of Unidade.

"Nicola got to rule this island and receive all the glory after I killed her once. She will pay greatly for what she did to me," said Tero in an extremely angry tone. He clutched his hands together and stretched his arms.

"You will get your revenge," reminded Alva Thoth. "Just do not let it get in the way of our ultimate goal. Remember, I will rule the world, and you will be king over this island if you can succeed at your quest."

As the two got closer to the tombs, Alva Thoth felt the magic of Karisma grow stronger.

"We are getting close," he mumbled to Tero. "There is the tomb. Ha, they tried to seal it, but it will not stop us. They are inside, waiting to ambush us. They think they are going to surprise us. They think I am alone. Little does precious Nicola know that this will be her last few minutes of life."

CHAPTER 48

The Battle Begins

Karisma bowed her head and fearfully said, "I can feel Alva Thoth outside of the tomb. We must be very careful in this fight. Take care of the flower at all costs. Alva Thoth cannot get his hands on the flower." Karisma handed the flower to Goran. "Use all of your strength to protect this."

Nicola grabbed her sword and looked at her friend and said, "I am here for you, Karisma."

Goran shoved the flower into Cass's hands and said, "Hold this. I have to protect our sister and my great-granddaughter." Goran grabbed his sword and swung it around to loosen up his shoulders.

Alva Thoth waved his staff over the entrance of the tomb, and the seal crumbled into small pebbles. Tero followed Alva Thoth into the tomb, keeping himself hidden until the right moment. Alva Thoth walked to the center of the room and found Nicola, Goran, and Karisma standing and waiting for them to enter.

"I have a surprise for you, Nicola." Tero appeared from behind Alva Thoth. Nicola's eyes lit up with great fear. Alva Thoth looked up and saw Ulric behind Karisma. "Hello, brother. I thought I felt something 'good' that I haven't felt in years. This will be fun, watching you and all of your creations die in one day."

"You will not take over the world," replied Ulric with a strong glare in his eyes.

Ulric lifted his staff and pointed it toward Alva Thoth.

"That will not work again. Your magic cannot touch me ever again. It is written into *your* prophecy. The time is up, you have lost."

Tero smiled at Nicola with his evil eyes and said, "It's your turn to bow to me. You will not survive this time."

Tero lifted his sword and leaned to attack Nicola. The attack knocked the sword out of Nicola's hands. She fell back, and with a swift kick to her stomach, she was knocked flat on her back. Tero smiled, and he looked into Nicola's fearful eyes. He lifted his sword to quickly kill Nicola, and as he started to jab it toward her heart, a sword swung and knocked Tero's sword from his grip. The sword flew across the tomb and landed with a loud cling. Tero looked up and saw Goran swinging his sword at him. Tero ducked under the attack and rolled on the ground to pick up his sword. He stood up to another challenge by Salem.

Tero said, "I will kill you both, and then I will finish you, Nicola. Our time will come."

Alva Thoth waved his staff, and a flash of lightning bolted from it and knocked Karisma, Ulric, and the brothers against the wall. The all hit the wall with a thunderous thud, and the flower fell from Cass's grip.

Alva Thoth picked it up, laughed, and said, "This was too easy. Kill her, Tero. Catch up with me when you are done."

Alva Thoth turned around and slowly left the tomb.

Tero walked to Nicola and kicked her in the side, knocking her back to the ground. He grabbed her hand and pulled her to her knees.

"Time to die," he whispered in her ear. "Too bad you didn't bow to my wishes. We could have ruled together."

Once more he kneed Nicola in the side of the head and placed the sword on the back of her neck. Nicola closed her eyes with bravery in her heart. He started to slash the sword toward Nicola. Cass, at the moment before the sword struck, tackled Tero to the ground. He punched Tero in the shoulder, and the sword fell from his grip.

"Get her out of here," Cass shouted to his brothers, who were just regaining their breath from hitting the wall with their back.

Goran picked her up over his shoulder and carried her out of the tomb. Salem and Karisma followed while Cass and Tero continued to fight. Cass was stronger and held Tero back from his quest. Tero eventually freed himself from the fight and sprinted out of the tomb, catching up to Alva Thoth.

"Did you kill her?" Alva Thoth asked.

"Not yet. The brothers saved her," he answered with disappointment.

Tero had blood coming out of his nose as he looked at Alva Thoth. Alva Thoth waved his hand over Tero's face, and the bleeding stopped.

"Your time will come. Be patient. We now have the flower. Nothing will be able to stop us now."

"Next time, I will be ready," exclaimed Tero, seeing images of Nicola in his thoughts.

"We have a quick quest to partake in. This will make you unstoppable in your fight with Nicola. Come with me," Alva Thoth commanded.

The two left the tomb of Unidade and started their new journey, this time with the flower in Alva Thoth's grasp.

CHAPTER 49

The End Is Near

Karisma quickly led the group to the banks of the dried-up Aurumton River. There she used what was left of her magic to heal Nicola. Karisma looked pale and faint as all of the magic left her body.

"What is wrong, Karisma?" asked Nicola.

Karisma answered slowly, "Nothing, just my magic becoming weaker as Alva Thoth becomes stronger. The flower kept my magic inside me. I will be fine. Don't worry about me. We need to get it back at all costs."

"Nicola, that was a very bad beating Tero gave you," Goran sadly said. He put his arm around her and hugged her tightly.

"He is a lot stronger than I remember him being," answered Nicola. "Thank you for saving me," she looked toward Cass and Salem, who were busy preparing their swords for another battle. "I can use some of my magic to help me in the next battle with Tero. I will stop him. I know what I am up against this time," she optimistically said.

Karisma, in deep thought, said, "There is a limited amount of magic left, especially without the flower in my control. The next battle *will be* the last battle. The end is near. There will be no more battles ever. I know what needs to be done, but I don't know if I will have the strength to do what I need to."

Tears fell from her eyes and rolled down her cheeks.

"What do you need to do?" sadly asked Nicola, knowing what Karisma would say, but afraid of the answer she would receive.

"I need to die with the flower. When I die, the magic will end. Alva Thoth is connected to the magic of the island. When the magic dies, he will die," Karisma answered. "He will not stop at ruling this island. He wants the world to be his. I will save the world at the cost of the island, our island."

Nicola, with tears filling her sky-blue eyes, cried, "There has to be another way to stop Alva Thoth. He seems to use his staff when he feels he is in trouble. Maybe we can take the staff and use it against him."

"Yes, that is true, but he is more powerful than we thought. He will not stop until his quest is done. There is no other way. I now see that," Karisma answered with a choked-up voice.

"Ulric, please help us find another way," pleaded Nicola. "I don't want my friend to die. I don't want this island to end. You created this island for good to rule. There is still good here, and it can be saved."

Ulric answered with all sincerity, "You always found the good in everything. That is why you were chosen to be the great queen, but Karisma is right, there is no other way. As long as Karisma and the flower are around, Alva Thoth will not stop in his quest to rule the world. I am sorry, Nicola, there is no other way."

Goran interrupted, "We will get the flower. We will stop at nothing. We will also hope for another solution, one that does not require the sacrifice of Karisma. We will hope for another outcome."

"We will rest here tonight. Tomorrow Alva Thoth will be stopped," Karisma said. She tightly hugged Nicola. "I wish there was another way. I am sorry, my friend. Together we will be strong."

"I understand," Nicola said, not letting go of Karisma's hug.

Nightfall seemed to happen quickly that night. The moon was dark, and the wind rustled through the trees. Sleep was hard to be found, but each got a little off and on through the night.

The sun rose the next morning. Nicola looked at the sunrise and saw Karisma sitting on a stump, looking toward the sky. Nicola walked over to Karisma and put her arm around her back and laid her head on Karisma's shoulder.

"The sunrises were always beautiful from this spot," Nicola softly said to Karisma. "I will find another way, one that you will not die Karisma. I promise you that I will do whatever I can."

"I know you will, but there is not another way. Evil has already won, and I will not let it take over the rest of the world," Karisma said with a saddened tone.

The girls were joined by the brothers.

"It is hard to believe that this used to be a great forest," said Salem.

"The river banks look lonely," said Cass. "I remember fishing and swimming here."

"We have not seen any other people. Remember when the road used to be crowded by the river?" added Goran.

"The island has changed. There are not a lot of people outside of the city. There is nothing left for them outside of their cities. You will find many places that battles occurred, but the armies are too small for battle now," Karisma said.

"The gold mines have to be left. There was an endless supply of gold," stated Goran.

"True, but the mines have been destroyed. The entrances are sealed, and there is no way to open the seals and reach gold," answered Karisma.

"People never learn. After the three kings, people turned to greed and power. After me, they did the same. They don't learn from the past history. They just want to rewrite it in their own way," said Nicola.

Ulric answered, "You speak wisely. From the time of Oton the Fierce, the lust for power and control have tainted the island. Only a handful were able to control the lust for power and keep peace and order. You four are the greatest of all the kings and queens. I thank you for keeping the island peaceful. Karisma, you did a great job in watching the island. You have nothing to be ashamed of. Evil won out because of me, but this can be stopped."

The group ate a small breakfast of the few nuts that could be found. The brothers sat off to the side, away from the rest, and talked. They agreed to make their final stand in the fields of Aurumton City, the same fields that Nicola defeated Tero many years before. The slow journey began without any words being spoken. Goran found an opportunity and snuck away and wandered off, alone.

CHAPTER 50

Evil Takes Hold

Alva Thoth and Tero made their way toward the emptied hot springs. The going was slow, so Alva Thoth changed into a red wolf and had Tero climb on his back.

"Hold on," Alva Thoth growled as he took one large leap, and the two landed on the sandy shore of the hot springs.

Alva Thoth changed back to his human form after they landed, and he looked at Tero, saying, "You are going to need more strength than you had before. Nicola will be no problem for you, but the brothers provided too much protection for you to overcome. I misjudged their strength, and that will not happen again." Alva Thoth swung his staff around in three circles in the air and then tapped his staff on Tero's head and Tero's strength more than doubled. "You are ready, but our job is not done."

"Thank you. I will not fail us this time. Nicola and the brothers will pay for what they did," Tero proudly exclaimed while he felt his strength grow inside.

Alava Thoth looked into the sky and mumbled something. He then waved his hands to the sky and drew a circle in the sand with his staff. The ground started to shake, and a tower grew out of the ground, just like a tree would. The tower resembled Karisma's, but it was crystal material that was tinted a reddish color. It was around one hundred feet tall with two windows. One looked over the dried hot springs, and the other looked toward the north, toward Silvager. There was a wooden door at the bottom that was opened.

Alva Thoth looked at the hot springs and spit into the dried-up hole. Boiling and steaming lava started to rise up and fill the springs. Tero could feel the heat from the new hot springs, but it did not seem to bother him as he was too focused on his task.

Alava Thoth waved his staff in the air and then dipped it in the now-full hot springs. The end of the staff started to burn, and Alva Thoth blew out the fire. He placed the smoking staff inside the tower, and a lady appeared in the doorway. The lady stood around six feet tall and was skinny. She had long black hair and reddish eyes. She wore a long scarlet dress that was lined in black. Her skin was pale, making the dress stand out. Her name was Prysma.

Alva Thoth commanded her, "You are to watch over this island and keep the magic of this flower safe. There will soon be people here to try to steal it. Do not let them. This is my only command to you, the only reason that I have created you."

Prysma answered, "Yes, my lord. It will be done." She bowed then took the flower from Alva Thoth, turned around, closed the door, and walked to the top of the tower.

Alva Thoth and Tero walked away and headed toward Kingsbridge Lake.

"The cowards are hiding," boasted Tero. "We have to find them before they can regroup."

Alva Thoth quietly answered, "I have a plan that will lead us to them." Alva Thoth changed back into the wolf. "Climb on my back, and we will accelerate my plan."

Tero climbed up on his back, and the two leaped to what was left of Karisma's tower. The pile of ashes was still smoldering while other ashes could be seen blowing around the lake. Alva Thoth landed and changed back to the old wizard.

"Why are we here at this old burning pile of garbage?" asked Tero.

"There is an old grave here, the grave of Karisma's brother, Az Rex. He was the first that I sent here with rage and a lust for power. He failed in his mission, and he was redeemed by his sister. We need to find that grave. I need something from it, something that will make Karisma suffer and become weaker," angrily answered Alva Thoth.

The two spent the rest of the night looking for the grave. As the sun rose, a beam of sunlight seemed to dance on some trees in the eastern part of the lake. Alva Thoth clapped his hands together, and he appeared at the spot the sunbeam landed.

"I found it," he yelled, showing some excitement for maybe the first time in his life.

He climbed between the trees and found a large pile of medium-sized rocks. Tero sprinted to the grave and helped Alva Thoth remove the rock pile. At the bottom of the rock pile was an ancient wrapped skeleton. Lying next to the skeleton was an old majestic sword that was rusted and falling apart. The sword was once sharpened on both edges, and the top was made into a hook-like shape. The handle had a wolf engraved into it.

Alva Thoth grabbed the sword and said, "This is what I was looking for."

"An old rusted sword? Why?" Tero laughed. "All this will do is fall apart when it strikes something."

Alva Thoth hit his staff on the sword. The sword started to glow with a blue light. The rust vanished from the blade. The sword became full of power.

"Az Rex never knew the true power of this sword. There is a hidden magic inside this sword. Az Rex used it as a weapon for battle, but never knew what the power held within it. This will make Karisma suffer, the sword of her brother. There is much power in the love of Karisma's love, and this was the item that killed Az Rex long ago. Her tears of love and grief fell on this sword, and her power and magic were inserted inside of it, unknown to her. This will be used to kill Nicola and the rest of the group. Use this to get your revenge."

Tero smiled at the thought of running the sword through Nicola's beating heart.

"Your wish will be done," he said with a large amount of some excitement.

"Nicola is the center of Karisma's strength. For me to kill her, you have to kill Nicola. Once Nicola dies, I will kill Karisma with the sword of her own brother." Alva Thoth laughed. He took the sword and pointed it toward the horizon. "The sword will lead us to our enemies." As Alva Thoth moved the sword, the glow changed from duller to brighter. "Follow the light, and we will find them."

The light pointed west, toward the ruins of Aurumton City, the same city that Tero burned many years ago. Alva Thoth changed into the wolf. Tero climb on his back, and the two quickly ran toward the ruins.

When they arrived, Tero climbed off the wolf's back and walked to the monument that Nicola had built for her parent's memory. He took the powerful sword of Az Rex and cut the monument in two.

"Hopefully Nicola will get my message that her time is *over*," he exclaimed to Alva Thoth, amazed at the power of the sword.

CHAPTER 51

The Final Battle Begins

In the distance, the brothers, Ulric, Karisma, and Nicola could be seen slowly making their way to the old courtyard.

"What happened to Goran's city and palace?" asked Salem, feeling empty at the loss of the city.

Nicola sadly answered, "When Tero attacked, he burned the city down. The palace is just ruins. I left it as ruins for a reminder to the people of what the lust for power brings. I built a monument for my parents after the battle was over. I had Unidade rebuilt to its former glory and ruled the island from one palace."

"The greed for power is a bad thing," sadly said Cass. "Goran fell into a trap, and Salem and I saved him, with the help of Karisma. There were consequences for the actions that happened."

Ulric stopped, fell on his knees, grabbed his heart, and said, "I feel my brother is very close, and he has grown in power."

The group stopped, and Nicola looked toward the ruins of the palace. She saw Tero standing where the main gate once stood.

"They are here," she yelled, pointing toward Tero.

"I am ready to stop this evil," yelled Salem.

Nicola looked around and said, "Has anyone seen Goran? I don't remember seeing him since we left Unidade."

Alva Thoth and Tero mythically and proudly walked to the field to meet their foes who were just entering the field, the same field that Nicola's rebels defeated Tero's powerful army many years ago. Karisma instructed to Cass and Salem that they get the flower no matter the cost. Nicola was ready for her showdown with Tero. This time she was mentally prepared for his strength. Ulric was ready for a fight with his brother. Karisma wanted to get the staff from Alva Thoth. The staff was what he used to unleash his power, and Karisma knew if she could get it, then her friends could have a chance at stopping the evil. She saw the sword that Tero was carrying and felt a great anger inside of her.

"How dare they go after the grave of my brother," she said to herself as her anger burned inside.

The brothers split, Cass going to one side of the field and Salem going to the other side of the field. Tero smiled and quickly sprinted at Nicola. Nicola was ready for him, holding a sword in both of her hands. She got a fast swing at him and cut his arm as he raised his sword for a quick kill. Ulric vanished and reappeared directly in front of his brother. Karisma vanished and appeared next to Ulric, reaching for the staff.

Tero swung the sword at Nicola again and again. This time Nicola was up to the challenge. Both duelers had cut marks on their hands and arms. Nicola was surprised at Tero's strength, but she surprised him with the two-handed sword-fighting, something she learned after their first battle many years ago. The dual lasted over fifteen minutes. Both Nicola and Tero were at the end of their physical limits. Nicola stepped back to avoid a slash by Tero and stepped on a rock, twisting her ankle and causing her to fall.

Tero looked her in the eyes and boasted, "Finally the break I needed to kill you."

CHAPTER 52

Goran's Adventure

Goran ran off from the group as they started their journey to the battlefield. He thought that Alva Thoth would go back to the place it all started, the magical hot springs. He ran as fast as he could, but he felt of out shape, which he attributed to being dead for hundreds of years.

As he slowed down, a dragon flew over and lifted him. The dragon flew to the sandy beach of the now-lava-filled hot springs. The black dragon with midnight-blue eyes looked at Goran and winked.

Goran whispered, "Thank you, Karisma."

He quickly glanced around and saw the tower standing on the beach. He also saw a vile filled with water sitting on the edge of the woods, the same kind of viles that were used to empty the water earlier. Goran knew Karisma's rule, but this was an extreme circumstance that was worth breaking the rules for. He playfully thought, *She can't punish the dead.* He had to save the island, the same island that he and brothers ruled over for many years.

Goran made his way to the tower and kicked the door off the hinges and walked up the steep spiral stairs. The door at the top of the stairs was open, and Goran found Prysma looking out the north window.

Prysma slowly turned around and looked at Goran and fell in love with the courage and honor she saw in him.

"Who are you?" she asked with wide eyes.

"I am Goran, the first king of Aurumton," he sternly answered.

Prysma smiled at him and said, "I am Prysma, keeper of the flower and ruler of the magic of the island."

Goran smiled back at her and said, "The flower? I need the flower to help my friends stop the evil from taking over. We are trying to save the island from falling into the new evil."

Prysma looked at Goran and waved her hand, and a lightning bolt shot at him. Goran jumped to the right and the bolt hit the wall.

"You cannot have the flower. It is mine to keep for my lord. Only he can have it."

Goran pleaded, "You don't understand. *Your lord*, Alva Thoth, is the evil one. He came here with one goal, to take the flower and use it to rule the island and then the world. He is on his way to kill the great rulers of the past and my sister, the one and true keeper of the island. She watched this island for seven hundred years until Alva Thoth was free of his banishment."

Prysma, feeling conflicted inside, said, "How do I know you are telling the truth? My lord told me to watch the flower, and like he said, you come here to steal it from me."

"I sense you are battling good and evil within your heart. Look deep down and use your magic to show you the truth. I feel your strength, and I know you can see right and wrong," begged Goran with tears filling his eyes.

Prysma shut her eyes and took a few deep breaths. She saw a vision of Alva Thoth robbing the grave of Az Rex. She saw the men and Alva Thoth taking the water out of the hot springs. She also saw Alva Thoth destroying the world. She took another breath and saw the three brothers, ruling together, with unity never seen before. She saw Nicola, the greatest of the rulers, ruling with honor, dignity, and a beauty that would never be matched. She also saw Karisma, sitting in her tower, keeping the magic and protecting the people of the island.

Prysma looked at Goran and started to cry, "Take the flower. Save your friends. I beg you."

She hugged Goran tight and kissed him on the cheek. She snapped her fingers, and Goran appeared on the battlefield, with the flower in his hands.

CHAPTER 53

The Battle Ends

Karisma met Alva Thoth in the middle of the field and said, "You will not take over the world. I *will* stop you."

"You have already lost." Alva Thoth said, smiling.

He raised his staff to Karisma's head and started to open his mouth when suddenly a lightning bolt knocked him off balance. She used the opportunity to grab the staff and eventually wrestle it from Alva Thoth grasp while Ulric was using a bolt of lightning from his own staff to pin Alva Thoth to the ground.

Alva Thoth looked defeated and puzzled as he looked at Karisma and said, "I have to admit, you surprised me, but I have a surprise for you. I don't have the flower. It is now protected from you. You will never have it." Alva Thoth pointed toward the battle of Nicola and Tero. "You might have me stopped temporarily, but your friend is about to die. When she dies, your life will be mine."

Salem started a sprint toward Tero.

"We have to save Nicola," he yelled toward Cass.

Tero looked at Nicola, kicked her in the ribs, and said, "Prepare to die. Your time is over, this time forever. Your friends will not be able to help you this time."

"Not yet," Nicola yelled as she slammed her foot into the side of Tero's knee.

Tero whelped with pain as his knee buckled backward, and Nicola stabbed the sword in her right hand into Tero's left shoulder.

Tero looked into her eyes, and he winced with the pain of the sword entering his shoulder.

"You have caused much grief to me. It is time for you tell your friends goodbye."

He swung his sword, and the handle of his sword hit Nicola's right hand. Her sword flew well out her reach. He kicked her left hand, and her smaller sword dropped to the ground. He grabbed her by the top of her hair and kicked her in the side of the head. Nicola looked up at him and took a deep breath. Tero smiled at her as he thrust his sword deep into her heart. Nicola fell over on her right side and bravely struggled as she took her last breath.

Salem reached Tero as his sword pierced her heart. With one swing of his sword to Tero's head, Tero fell and died the moment before Nicola took her final breath. Cass, following closely, held Nicola in his arms and cried out loud.

Goran ran up to the battlefield in a panic and saw Cass holding Nicola. He sprinted toward them, showing that he had the flower.

"Where is Karisma? She will know what to do," Goran demanded.

Cass pointed to the center of the field. Goran grabbed his sword with his right hand and held the flower with his left hand and charged toward Alva Thoth.

Alva Thoth saw Goran holding the flower, and he looked at Karisma and whispered in her ear, "Impossible. Give me *the flower,* and all this eternal pain will be over. You lost your magic. Now let me end it for you. Your friend is dead. She will never take another breath."

Karisma, distracted by Alva Thoth's words, lost her grip that was holding him down. Alva Thoth swung his hand and Tero's sword, the sword of Az Rex, shot across the field and struck Ulric in the chest. Ulric fell to his knees and dropped his staff. Alva Thoth swung his hand again, and the sword flew to him.

Goran threw the flower to Karisma, and he used his mighty sword and struck Alva Thoth's hand, cutting it off with one swing. Az Rex's sword fell in front of Karisma.

Karisma looked at Nicola and picked up the flower.

She grabbed Az Rex's sword and bravely boasted, "You are right, it is over. You will never harm anyone ever again."

"You know that you cannot kill me," proudly said Alva Thoth. "I am too strong for you to kill."

Karisma humbly replied, "I know that I cannot kill you, but I can *stop* you."

Karisma placed the flower over her own heart and used Az Rex's sword to stab the flower, going through her own heart.

Alva Thoth, with a surprised look, yelled, "*No!* What are you doing?"

"When the flower and I die, the magic dies. You now have nothing," Karisma faintly responded while she was taking small and painful breaths.

Karisma's breathing became more difficult. She looked at her three brothers. They looked back and tearfully smiled. Ulric held his head in hands and moved his lips, trying to say something.

Alva Thoth, as Karisma began to weaken and the flower lost its petals, turned to dust and fell to the ground.

"It is finished. The time of the island has come to an end," Karisma said softly.

Ulric, choking on his words, smiled at Karisma and said, "You are the wisest wizard to ever walk on the earth."

When he was done talking, he vanished into thin air, never to be seen or heard again.

Each of the brothers took time to quickly hug Karisma. They each said a thank-you for what she had done for them, and they each said their tearful goodbyes. A large group hug ended with the brothers disappearing to nothing.

Karisma stumbled to where Nicola's body was lying.

With tears in her eyes, she said, "I already miss you, my friend. I love you," she whispered and fell next to Nicola.

Karisma held Nicola in her arms as she took her final breath.

As Karisma died, the island began to sink into the ocean. The sandy shores disappeared. The old forest became engulfed by the rushing water. The mountains began to be covered. After a few minutes, the whole island was gone, except the tallest peak still stuck out of the ocean six inches. There a flower grew, a flower that was about two hands tall, with midnight-blue petals and a glowing red center. The flower seemed to look at the sun. A wolf's howl was heard in the distance, and a large glowing red book appeared next to the flower.

The End

ABOUT THE AUTHOR

Chris was born in Wichita Falls, Texas, and now resides in Westfield, Indiana. Chris graduated from Air Academy High School in Colorado and has a bachelor's degree in marketing from the University of Phoenix. He is married and has two sons and two daughters. This is Chris's first book. He is an avid fan of historical baseball and the Indianapolis 500.

CPSIA information can be obtained
at www.ICGtesting.com
Printed in the USA
LVHW030452301121
704812LV00002B/135